Sylvia Littlegood-Briggs
Wild Marjoram Tea

[bc14b]

First published in 2021 by Broodcomb Press

www.broodcomb.co.uk

ISBN 978-1-9996298-7-8

Cover image *Salt Flowers* [bc15a]

Printed in England by T J Books Limited, Padstow, Cornwall

Sylvia Littlegood-Briggs
Wild Marjoram Tea

Past tears are present strength.

George MacDonald, *Phantastes*

I dreamed a vivid dream
of a doorkey broken in the lock,
end lost in the works, yet the act
of snap had made the remains *gleam*.

J.M. Walsh, *A Journal*

In a way not fully clear to me,
this book is for Jason Retallick,
in memoriam—

I

Tom Stuckey was a presence on the school bus, quiet and awkward, prone to fingering his hands into his sleeves until the ends of his jumpers were ragged. Polly knew his face, but he was no object of curiosity or wariness or desire. He was simply present, the boy who lived halfway down the lane that led to the hamlet of Cinderhill.

One Saturday afternoon, however, Tom was in Polly's living room when she arrived home after working on an end-of-year project with a feared classmate in Cubton. Tom's mother, Emese, had been crossing the Pook Farm field opposite, heading back from shopping via a short cut. The local newspapers would call it an animal attack, but Polly knew before being told by the adults that this was unlikely. There were no calves in the field. Even if there had been, the cows would have known the woman by sight. In all likelihood, the herd moved alongside Emese as she was walking, perhaps drawn by the scent or sound of something she'd bought in the town. At first, as they pressed in, there'd have been breathless disbelief—

"She'd have known," Polly's mother Jo said, more annoyed than upset. "At some point, she'd have known what was happening."

The woman's shopping had been found distant from the body, and Polly, even at fifteen, knew in her gut and bones this was where panic had set in, shopping abandoned when it became clear those dumb bone-crates of milk and shit had an insistent and stupid power in their being that was lethal precisely because it was oblivious. Cows were all weight and no mind; they simply existed. The shift from concern to survival would have been fast, seconds only. As the cows moved in, their power would have cut off her air and pressed her into the centre of the herd until she was knocked off balance, or simply fell, and she went under their feet. The cows were Holsteins, each around a hundred stones in weight, and Tom's mother went under their feet.

She was still breathing when found, shallow as her chest was crushed. Her skull was open at the rear, yet she managed to speak. An ambulance man heard her say, *There were riders. Sharp riders.* Then she was dead.

The house where Polly lived was half a mile further up the road from Cinderhill, on the crossroads where one lane led to Claypits and the other to the Pook Farm hard by Hundredwood. No one wanted to be at the Stuckey house, so everyone gathered in their old farmhand's cottage, Polly's parents in the kitchen with the police, her mother attempting to nail down *next steps* and *contingencies* while her father tried to sedate Alan Stuckey with sloe gin.

Polly and Tom sat alone in the living room. She could hear the adults talk through the door that had never closed properly. Her mother was extracting splinters of fact with the hot needle of her attention. The police wouldn't be leaving for some time, which meant Polly was stuck with the boy, yet she'd nothing to say, no wherewithal. She didn't understand why he looked like he'd done something wrong, as if his own grief was a precious vase he'd knocked over in his clumsiness and he was waiting for the yelling to start. Long minutes of sitting and staring passed before he spoke—

"My dad can't drink."

"Oh."

"Your dad is giving my dad drink. My dad can't drink."

Polly took a while to understand the meaning of this. Once Tom had begun talking he seemed to want to go on but not know how.

"There's blood in the field," he said, quiet and with no inflection. "In the mud. There's blood in the field."

Polly said nothing. She kept her attention on him, unwavering because she felt her will was the only thing stopping the boy from crying, which she did not want. She'd experienced the same feeling the one time she'd flown. Only her will and attention kept the aeroplane in the air. The flight was long, yet she had to stay awake. For her, at this moment in her life, a boy crying and a plane crashing were disasters of similar magnitude.

Her father walked Alan Stuckey home when the police left. "I don't want him to be alone," he said, "and I think the boy should stay here."

Her mother agreed, hesitant because their cottage was tiny and she saw the thought the boy might have to share Polly's room occur to her daughter at the same time as it crossed her own mind. She felt the girl's panic physically, tactile as a jolt of static electricity.

"We'll have supper," she said. "I'll make cheese on toast. Polly, put a match to the fire. Tom——." She paused as the boy didn't register his name. "Tom, you'll be okay on the couch here. I'll get a duvet."

It was dark now, and when he lifted his head, his eyes remained in shadow. "Her blood's in the field," he said, still quiet and flat. "Is someone going to clear it up?"

Polly's mother made a move towards him. Tom read her intention and stood, putting the arm of the couch between them. He would not be held by her. She might have made it if she'd seized him, but Polly knew her mother was too orderly for that. Her emotional intent was always oversignalled, the tick of her calculations audible from a distance.

"Polly, put a match to the fire. Tom, shoes off. Cheese on toast."

The evening was strange without her father. Polly longed to have gone with him to slip the oddness of his absence, even if it meant putting herself in proximity to the massive grief of Alan Stuckey. Somehow that would have been more manageable, because it was not hers to deal with. She'd already realised she was expected to take care of Tom. Polly didn't know how it had happened, but they'd all swiftly slid into costumes and scenes cut to fit them before they were even aware of the play: the men forced into an emotionally blunderful two-hander, her mother versus all forces of authority, Polly and Tom as tongue-tied juvenile leads. She knew this as keenly as she knew none of them had auditioned for their part.

They ate. All through the Saturday treat, an episode of *C.A.T.S. Eyes* called 'Freeze Heat', she focused on Tom as the dark gathered, the only light in the small front room the low fire and the television screen. The boy was impenetrable, exotic in grief, his presence an annoyance. She couldn't take her eyes from him, yet she wanted him to vanish from sight. Despite going to bed as soon as she reasonably could, her thoughts picked up the vibrations of his unseen, unheard bereavement engine. Her room was above the living room, and after she heard the indistinct murmuring of her mother before she too went to bed, the silence from below was a chimney of noise running right through her head. She could not stop thinking of him down there, a boy in her home, strange and limby as a spider spinning grief-black silk all over the walls of her house.

She could not sleep. Tom was too disturbing, and more disturbing was the suffocating presence of the death itself. Polly was a country girl and had been conversing happily with the cows in the fields since before her memories began. Cows were eyelash and udder, great velvet flanks and winter morning steam, muscular tongues and stinks. For them to have crushed Tom's mum to death was a closed, malevolent fact she could not turn her mind from because it challenged all she understood of reality. Cows she'd walked among, invisible but for her feet as she was short, had turned killers, first robbing Emese's breath with their pressing bulk and then the integrity of her body with their hooves. Somehow worst of all, although she could not articulate it, was that every actor in the death was female. A quality of this truth undid her in ways that thieved her breath, and every time she needed sleep her consciousness of how grateful she was for breath itself shook her awake. Nothing as shocking had happened since a neighbour's child had drowned in the cesspit when he was six years old and she'd caught sight of the hollowed out parents.

Sleep would not come. Her body taunted her. She was thirsty and needed the loo but both required her to walk downstairs and through the room where Tom slept. In the early hours she got up and found her notebook. She'd become obsessed with Cocteau Twins lyrics and listened pen in hand trying to decipher the river of syllables that tumbled from the singer's mouth. *Victorialand* was newly out and her cassette was already arthritic with use. The moon was quarter full, cloud at scud across the darkness. The stars were clear here, few houses, none lit, and the moors held a line of grey light to the north. She stared upwards and listened to the music, not hearing anything she could identify as human speech but finding worlds of comfort there all the same.

She was still awake when the spill of light from the open front door lit the ground beneath her window. There was no sound. The boy was taking pains not to be heard. She didn't even hear the click as the front door closed. Face to the glass she watched Tom walk to the crossroads, but instead of turning right towards his house, he climbed the gate into the field and vanished into the darkness.

Polly dressed quickly. Dawn was approaching so once in the field she saw Tom standing not too distant, his silhouette forming a thin wintered tree against the lightening sky. With a shock she saw the police tape already torn from its metal hook pole and blowing in the wind. She had no idea the death had happened so close to her house, so close to the woman's own home.

"I saw you come out," she whispered.

Tom didn't move. "It happened here," he replied. He pointed to the earth where gouges were driven into wet mud, set overnight into scars. Most were trenches driven in by a sliding hoof, but some were cloven wells here and there where the cattle had stood. "Blood," he said.

Polly could see it then: a line of black and two filled ink wells where the blood had pooled and cooled. His mother's blood.

She'd no idea where she found the confidence. Afterwards she viewed the move with startlement and a little fear, yet she, five foot nothing, took the hand of this boy closing in on six foot and held it as he stood there and wept, and when minutes later he asked—

"What happens now?"

—she squeezed tighter and said, "I don't know."

Tom stayed with them for the best part of a week, and by the time he returned to his father's house down the road, he and Polly were knotted in each other's lives and emotions in a way that bewildered them both. Both only children, shock and grief had sidestepped any notion of attraction and settled them as siblings. She overheard her mother ask about their relationship, "Is that strange?"

"No," her father replied. "They take themselves out of themselves."

"That's a good sentence," said her mother with disdain, but Polly knew what he'd meant. The two had connected, and it was an enclave of vulnerable support. Polly was lonely, and now she was not. Tom was abandoned, and now he was not.

Without close relatives, the innards of other families were a mystery to her, or rather she assumed they were the same as hers: a mother like an emotional clerk, an eye on the balance sheet of human accountability; her father intent on her joy with an inhibited playfulness like a frog caught under glass, gleefully hopping but essentially airless. Walking Tom home that first time, she was upset to find his house bereft of any parental attention at all. Alan truly seemed not to see either of them, but particularly his son. Polly felt invisible, a sense she knew caused Tom a wordless pain but that she felt as freeing.

At home she was the bullseye in the target of her mother's driver *Let's work* and her father's driver *Let's play*. Despite this attention she was lonely. Attention of one sort or the other was wearying. Mostly she wanted to be left alone. Her mother burrowed around her period like she was rootling for the egg; her father clowned around as if he could magic it out of all existence. Her mother invested her homework with the weight of the future, what qualifications might buy her; her father tried endlessly to fun it up or distract her with play. Polly was never happier than when a book reached out and got her in its nails. There were two tribes of pictures in the house: Polly achieving and Polly playing. Neither of them was comfortable to her because when she looked into her own eyes she saw a stranger.

At Alan Stuckey's house, it was as if Tom lived in the walls, a mouse deliberately overlooked because to notice him would mean action needed to be taken. He was a boy who didn't exist.

"Is he okay?" she asked one day. "Can someone help him?"

Tom shrugged. "He was like this before. He's always been like this. At least he's not drinking."

He acted as if he was fine with this situation – with everything – but in glimpses Polly saw the yearning to connect with his father, to share memories of his mother, to engage in that delicate human dance where emotions allow themselves to touch, just briefly and shyly for moments of reassurance that the other is still there, but father and son lived in different worlds.

"It's like we're ghosts in this house," she said once.

Tom replied, "We're each other's ghosts. And the medium died in that field."

At once he looked pleased and ashamed, ashamed at the bluntness of his words, but pleased with how they'd come out.

There was a benefit to this lack of parental care. Tom was altogether a freer spirit than she. They dawdled after school, sharing time in each other's houses. Although they did not mix in school, one afternoon she saw him heading into Cubton town centre and followed him. If he was surprised when she finally showed herself to him, he didn't show it, and they spent the afternoon playing pool, *men* at the other tables and rowy music on the jukebox. The room was dark, smoke lying in lines under the lights, and heavy with the smell of cigarettes and wet leather jackets. The place scared her as it radiated danger, yet it was the girls and women there who were more frightening to her than the boys and men, who seemed to like that she was small and had to stand on a box to take shots when the white was in the middle of the table. In a slightly unclear way, she understood Tom was afraid of the men in the pool hall because they were a different breed to him. Somehow, in this place that belonged to him as male, she was the safer—

Walking home in the early summer evening, she sensed the edges of an elemental understanding. In company – and in no way an *actual* sense – Tom stood a little forward of her physically, not acting, but present if he was needed; in a similar way she stood a little forward of him emotionally, not acting, but present if she was needed.

Most of the time they spent together was in the countryside. Alan Stuckey never curbed the boy's freedom, and Polly had new freedom in saying she was with Tom. The idea she had taken the boy under her wing pleased her parents, and their friendship undid all parental concern. Polly was surprised how completely they stepped away from protection once Tom was a fixture.

A habit he had was of walking at night. At first she was nervous, but after a time she loved the idea they were out in the darkness. The first time they went out was a full moon night. Tom took her on his usual path, down into Cinderhill, creeping past the few houses then round Pook's Wood. To her left were the moonlit fields, cattle lowing in the grass. The sight of them brought to mind a conversation she'd overheard her parents having about Emese's last words, *There were riders. Sharp riders.* Her father was wondering what she'd meant, and her mother had replied, "Her brain was damaged, Tony. She didn't know what she was saying."

To cover her nerves, she told Tom, "John Westcott said cows like to go out at night. He's seen them choose an open door over food."

They stood and listened to the low complaint of the animals, one of them occasionally loosing a booty moo into the night air. "They're warning against threat," he said. "Talking to each other. I don't know what the threat is."

"It's us. We're in the shadow of the trees. They know we're in the shadows. Cows can see better in the dark than we can. They have super-openable eyes."

"*Superopenable.* Such a swot. With your words."

She laughed. The loudness of the sound got into her heartbeat. "I grew up around here," she said. "I'm not a towny like you."

The woods to their right were all gloom. They kept an even distance, yet Polly had the sense a creature was tracking them just inside the tree line, fleet and silent. A creature that was somehow handsy and mean. With the chill in the air and the high white moon, she felt exposed. In the night, fields she knew became strange and distant. She felt as if she'd walked into the wrong class at school, the room familiar but the faces gazing back at her strangers.

She said this to Tom but he didn't quite hear her—

"I know where we are," he said.

She wanted to reply, *I know where we are too but it isn't here. Where we are is different at night.*

They cut through Pook's Wood at the lane that led into Cubton. The raucous pub in the distance was as alien as the fields had been. Being in the woods at night was an astonishment to Polly. Without light falling in from the day above, the canopy was firm as a church roof, enclosing and holding in its own sacred weight. The coolness was the coolness of church stone. Midway through the cut, they stopped and sat. Neither spoke. The sounds of the wood became all. A hoot sounded and Polly knew it was a tawny owl—

"In Germany," she whispered, "tawny owls don't *to-whit to-woo*, they call *komm mit komm mit. Come with me come with me.*"

Tom opened his mouth in mock terror at how ominous this sounded, but he didn't look at her. He sat hunched over, hands deep in greatcoat pockets, staring at the ground and listening, listening.

Polly listened too. The great night was alive around them, massive and breathing, the leaves fussing with bright noises firing her nerves. The soft tread of foxes, the cubs only now leaving the vixen to go out on their own. Night birds chirped and faffed high in the branches, and she knew bats would be muttering all around her, an insistent and necessary speech humans could not hear to navigate a space identical to their own yet entirely separate.

Polly breathed, aware of her lungs and their thousandfold branches. The scents were getting inside her. Tom was right: she was a swot. She knew the smells of the earth, soil microorganisms snoozing out *geosmin* and, underneath, one of her favourite ever words: *petrichor.* The smell of rain, except the aroma was more than this. *Petrichor* was an expression of how rain made the whole world new in every sensory way.

Tom intuited the way her thoughts were going—

"The trees are talking to each other too. In smells."

"Are they talking about us, do you reckon?"

"Of course. Wouldn't you?"

They came out of Pook's Wood where Hundredwood started. A white barn owl quartered the field to the north, a ghost presence in the night. A river divided the two woods and the difference was stark. A boy had gone missing over in Hundredwood some years before, never to be found, and the authorities had cut down the trees right up to the water, an inexplicable and needless violence to some and the cause of considerable ill feeling. Many residents of Cinderhill called it Murdered Wood.

"It looks like the moon," she said.

"My dad said they're going to replant. Might have already started."

To Polly, Hundredwood in the moonlight was evidence of an atrocity. The light was silver and the tops of the boles cut level with the earth looked like hundreds of enormous coins cast on the ground as far as she could see. The place was foreign, sinister. Tom felt it too. Crossing the river at the wooden bridge, the water a grey mutter underneath, he turned hard right to avoid stepping into the field of stumps, taking the lane up to the crossroads and her cottage.

Tom never spoke of his mum to Polly. Her mother encouraged her to eke it out of him – "It's therapeutic," Jo said – but Polly knew instinctively this would not work. He'd not grown up with that hot needle of attention probing his skin, and she knew he'd flinch and flee at the intrusion. She waited him out, glad of his company.

The more he loosened, the more she found him cheeky and funny. His dour Ian-McCullochiness shifted to reveal someone adventurous and enthused, much like herself, she thought. They caught buses into town occasionally – record shopping – but out in the country was where they were happiest. Looking back, nothing meaningful had ever been said or done but whole worlds of mutual understanding had been reached.

Nor was their talk free from adolescent conceit and paranoia. They talked wonderingly of the Bavarian Illuminati, haunted houses, the chance the next Pope would be the Antichrist, the house over near the Maerker Estate where a doctor turned burn victims into ghouls, the Holy Grail and *Chariots of the Gods*. As with any two humans, one (Polly) was the more factual, bookish, aligned to the light, and the other (Tom) was credulous, lulled by mysticism, drawn to the shadow.

An instance of this came in the summer after school had broken up. Polly made moth water from alcohol and brown sugar, and after dark they walked to the edge of the forest near where they'd first sat and inhaled the forest night. She painted the solution on the trees at head height. When the moths came, she and Tom watched as they fed, an act Polly insisted (wrongly) was called *lollygagging*. She'd brought a torch to watch the moths, but Tom had filled his pockets with candles. The less directed light of the candle lit him – lit them both when she abandoned her torch – and when they got close to the patch of sugar stink on the tree, they were alone in a moon of light, impenetrable darkness enclosing them, staring at a moth that seemed the size of her fist and whose wings disturbed the candle's flame.

"You can use wine ropes as well," she whispered. "Cook some rope in wine and sugar then hang the ropes over branches."

Tom was open in wonder. The moth's proboscis was golden in the candlelight, moving over the surface of the wood. The sound of its wings could almost have been the ribbed purr of a cat.

"We made a light trap once," she said. "Hundreds of moths in there. They looked like they were wearing grey coats. Like butterflies behind the Iron Curtain."

"Goth butterflies. Little flying Ian Curtes."

"Not a Goth."

Tom didn't reply. She noted how deft he was at moving the candle away when the moth began to be drawn to the light more than the food. Tom was sensitive to this, managing to keep the moth feeding, only pulling back when more moths came. It was beautiful to be moonlit, interacting with the creatures of the night, but she understood her knowledge didn't pull him as she wanted it to. It wasn't that she wanted to be thought clever, but she did want him to see her, and she was uncomfortable with the silence. Yet he was happy with the silence, and it was a comfort that she could not follow him into. Mothing took him to a place of wonder he entered into more completely than her, and she suspected it was because he was less hindered by knowing. Words were weights; facts were weights. If you were airborne, they hindered your flight.

She watched his face against the bark and wondered how they'd both look to an outsider. *Mythic*, she decided, like a scene from folklore, a winged creature built of dust and enchantment hovering between them at the centre of their gaze—

"It can fly at twelve miles per hour," she told him. "Twice as fast as you can run."

The summer holidays opened up new possibilities. Polly had always been expected to pay her way in the family. She helped out at the estate agency her father was a partner in, Gloyn and Briggs, putting much of the money away for a future car. There was little to do bar xeroxing and arranging viewings over the phone.

The agency had taken over a planning office going back centuries and had a room full of old maps, drawings and blueprints. The two men had been trying to get the local council to house the documents but neither they nor the settlements wanted them. Polly liked looking at the brittle paper and the rusted clips holding old photos to the top of the plan or map. The mustiness of the paper and the depth of the print entranced her. She could see the physical force needed to press in the images on these old plans and drawings, feel the ridges with her fingertips.

Happiest of all was finding a map with names she knew. Tinford, Rackenwell, Hollow Thomas. She traced some of the more interesting places they might visit. Few were within walking distance, but Tom had already said she could borrow his mother's bike, a lending Polly was still uncertain about accepting. In a way she couldn't explain, taking the dead woman's bike was close to wearing her clothes. Intellectually, the thought was foolish; emotionally—

Walkable was Rackenwell, south of Pook's Wood. A mile outside of the village, she had found a drawing of a cluster of houses that didn't exist. She asked Mr Gloyn about it, and he'd told her the new road went through there.

"The peninsular bypass." He pulled a more recent map from the shelf. "See here. It goes south right through. They must have compulsory purchased the land and kicked the residents off. The bastards."

Polly and Tom walked there over the fields. They never talked much when walking. Tom always seemed lost in thought, and Polly was alive to her surroundings. Just getting to the south of Pook's Wood took the best part of an hour, and she could smell their packed lunches and their sweat by the time they heard the road in the distance. The sun was high. She had her shirt tied around her waist and Tom was down to his T-shirt.

"It should be about here," she said, taking the tracing paper copy from her pocket.

Ahead was the bypass, not busy but alien, intrusive, an obscenity of a horizon when all before it was delicate meadow, buttercup, corncockle, cow parsley, columbine, orchid. She loved saying the names in her head, then the words ended and there was only the bypass—

"Maybe those trees?" he asked, pointing a little way down. "You said they were in trees."

Nestled in the woods, which did not look healthy, was a dip that contained three cottages, all ruins. The road passed hard by, raised over a culvert – invisible if driving on the road – which allowed a stream to pass underneath. Once this place had been three tiny cottages by a stream, doubtless farmhands' dwellings. Without the road, they would have been hidden in the trees, a small community. At night, the cottages would have been sunk in the dark of the copse, water nattering outside all night long, nothing but fields and stars all around. Polly could think of nothing more glorious.

"I'm going to cool my feet. Cool my heels," said Tom.

While he took off his shoes and socks, Polly looked around the houses. They were just walls now, one house complete but the other two with only the chimney and a couple of half-hearted walls flanking the hearth. Even in the complete house, empty of everything, the cottage was tiny. Polly's home was of a later era, a two-up-two-down with a later extension for a loo, but even that looked a manse compared to this.

"It was burned," she called to Tom as she traced the inner blackened walls. "They must have set fire to them to destroy them."

"I hope they didn't burn the occupants out."

"No. It was the sixties. It would've been a little old lady and a little old man."

"They'd have gone into a home then." He looked at her through the ruined window. "It would have broken their hearts," he said. "This water is cold."

It surprised Polly there was no floor, not a shred left even though in the well of the house she saw bits of old wooden window frames and crockery that must have belonged to the house. It was as if the floor had been eaten from below, which for all she knew was possible. Now the living quarters were solely the fief of creepers, weeds, bushes, the occasional wild flower blown in from the meadow and thirsting for light.

Tom crunched around outside. "Can I have my sandwich?" he asked.

"I'm not the sandwich police."

It was pleasant to eat by the water. Tom was sweating but he wouldn't take off his shirt. Polly noticed he ate in a strange fashion, a way that felt learned. He'd not bite from the body of the sandwich but tear off a manageable piece he'd then put whole into his mouth.

"Weird the inside is the same as the outside," he said, nodding into the house that had all the walls intact. "All of our houses are like that underneath the decorating. It's hard to believe they stay upright at all."

Polly pointed to the sunken squares halfway up the walls. "Weird those holes were all that kept the bedroom floors up," she said. "That's where the roof beams went then the floorboards went on top."

"Weird there's no floor. Where did that go?"

"Eaten from below," she said and laughed when she saw his face, as if his mind was throwing up a toothed horror under the soil.

Later, when Polly thought of these moments as an adult, she marvelled at how little was spoken and how comfortable she was with Tom. In retrospect, there wasn't a boy she met for whom a part of her – a bodily part of her – did not scan with carnal radar for sexual possibility, and a significant part of her comfort with Tom was that her radar did not ping with him. More curiously, she understood at a basic level he lacked this same ping with her. Yet it seemed simplistic to see this as a consequence of their first meeting being in grief. It was more than that; it was a sibling separateness of being interested in the same things, which in all truth was nothing deeper than comfort in being out in nature rather than obsessed with books, or music, or film. They clung to each other because the friendship – in the countryside where few children were around or like them – was the more vital part of their relationship.

They rarely spoke but they seemed to share so much. He could read her dissatisfaction with her parents, which was hard for her to articulate given his situation. To complain would have felt ungrateful in the extreme. To have two parents at all was a luxury, but to have one who cared so much about her intellectual well-being as her mum, and as much about her creative well-being as her dad, was a wonder, and to moan that neither cared about what she actually *wanted* felt obscene. In return, she knew without being told his feelings of helplessness about his father. Work was losing patience with Alan's productivity – he was a site contractor – and at home he slipped into a listless torpor that looked like nonexistence. No one seemed to be able to help—

"He needs to snap out of it," her mother said once. "I know it's hard, but he's got responsibilities. Thank God for Polly with the boy."

"It's not that simple," replied her father quietly. "Where he is—." He shook his head. "It's not a place where deciding-to-be-better is a possibility." He spoke carefully. *He's speaking on tiptoe*, Polly thought, and she knew he was creeping through a minefield where the mines were female scorn bombs. "You're asking the man to turn the handle in a room that has no doors."

Polly understood without speaking how keenly Tom was listening outside that room with no doors, *and* how little he could admit to his listening.

The day of the ruined houses was one Polly would later wonder at. As an adult she was often ashamed at how selfward-turned she'd been as an adolescent, and the knowledge this was true for all – that it belonged to adolescents in general, not her alone – somehow never translated to acceptance. An anomaly in this, and one that spoke to her and Tom's relationship, happened that day.

There was a bank around the back of the ruined cottages, fallen glass on the ground in front where the bank had collapsed in places. "I think it's a dump," Tom said as he toed into it.

Over an hour they got dirty digging through it, spurred on by extraordinary finds, extraordinary not in any sense of monetary value but in terms of age. They turned up dozens of old apothecary bottles, some beautiful colours and each stamped with imperial measurements and the names of old chemists. Some were tiny and all had smooth lips.

"They'd've been corked," she said. "No screwtops. They're so old."

The majority were also curiously rectangular, the glass thick and heavy. The most beautiful were the blue ones. They changed the world. The thickness of the glass distorted when held up to the eyes, and the blue turned the world both dark and light. Flowers in particular glowed depending on their colour. Tom was staring through one with the name *Tresidder* moulded sideways down the length of the bottle. The way the light bent around the letters made the world seem to move as though light itself was crawling over the undergrowth and flowers.

"It's like the plants are filled with maggots," he said. "Look at the rosehips. They're black."

He passed the bottle over to her. The rosehips were dark yet other flowers seem to glow, bright points of light so contrasting to the surrounding darkness that they looked like stars in the night sky.

"I read that in the nineteenth century, there was a craze for blue light. People would have blue light rooms where all the glass was blue."

"How come?"

Polly shrugged. "Blue glass cured them. Or the light did. I think they sat in blue glass rooms and their hair grew back." He laughed hard at this. "No, seriously. The whole world went bonkers about it. Said it cured their bad backs, colds——. I don't know what else." She paused. "This is so amazing."

There was a fallen tree on the other side of the stream. Shoeless, they arranged their treasures on the trunk. It was astonishing how much had been dumped in the bank: bottles, clay pipes, fragments of ceramic jars. They washed the mud off in the stream and set them in a line. The bottles were so *made* she was happy simply to look at them, their imperfections and the bubbles caught in the thick glass. Some of the brown ones were so dark as to be almost non-transparent. Looking through them turned the day to night. But the blue ones she adored——

Tom hauled out a kettle the size of a human head, rusted through here and there but the thick base still weighty. It was filled with mud.

"Careful of the metal," she said. "Don't cut yourself on old metal."

Polly didn't understand the appeal of the kettle to Tom. It was dirty and the rust repulsed her. Rust always reminded her of scabs just before they were ready to peel off. At the back of the kettle, where the long loop of the handle attached, the rust had eaten through to reveal an animal bone.

"It must have crawled in and died," she said.

Tom emptied the kettle. The mud was wet, slumping onto the ground like blancmange. Delicately, Tom picked through it, taking out things of worth and washing them in the stream before putting them on the fallen trunk. Two tiny bottles, one of red glass her heart reached out for. A spoon, a skull, a strange metal bowl like an egg cup without a stand. A button and two old tuppence coins that looked foolishly large, then a sixpence.

"Ace," he muttered.

Polly couldn't see what he'd found. Once he'd rinsed the last object clean, he set it at the end of the treasure row: a gold pouring jug, small, about the size of the individual milk jugs used in cafés. The jug was wholly rounded, sitting like a chick on the smallest of bases, its lips sticking out sweetly.

"It looks like it's sulking," she said. "I love it."

"Me too."

The haul standing along the log comprised about twenty items, most bottles. Any bottle incomplete or with a chip had been discarded, and the only bone kept was the skull, which was about the size of Tom's thumb but that neither could identify. At the end was the gold jug.

The two took turns to pick what they wanted, and in later life Polly marvelled at how this moment played out. Neither of them picked the true treasure, the little gold jug. They were right in the heart of that period of human development where the only air is the air of self-regard, and yet neither took the jug. He chose the skull; she chose the red bottle. Each picked one of the blue bottles, Tom the larger one. She took the spoon; he took the bone button. A coin each. Her, the small eggcup bowl; him, the one clay pipe that was most whole, the bowl intact with a good length of stem—

In the end, two things were left: a clear glass bottle and the small gold jug. It was Polly's turn, and she picked the bottle. She wanted him to have the gold jug, and yet the way the divvying had played out, it was clear they both felt the same way.

The moment was deeply significant for Polly. She believed it had changed her. She had behaved against her grain. Childhood changes can happen in a heartbeat. The girl who walked back with her haul tied into her shirt was a different person from the one who'd walked out. When she got home, she put the red bottle and the blue bottle side by side on her sill where they could catch the light. In every house she ever lived, those bottles were always there within sight of a window.

"Such a good day," he said as they parted on the lane. "What's next?"

What was next was a property she'd found in the middle of Pook's Wood. It had an innocuous name on the old map she'd found at the estate agency. *The Grange*. What drew her attention was that there was a graveyard on the property, marked clearly on the map as *cem.* and hard by the house.

"Was this a church?" she asked.

Mr Gloyn got his tiny eyes close to the old map. "No," he replied. "Not in the middle of woods. Churches around here tended to be sited near yews. That's where the pagans the Christian buggers wanted to convert worshipped." He paused. "I think that's the Littlegood place."

"Someone lives there?"

"I assume so."

Polly put her head next to his. He smelled of cheese and books. "Where's the road? There'll be a road."

Mr Gloyn tapped the map. "Here-ish. Back then it would've been a dirt track. I expect there's a tarmacked road there now."

Yet there wasn't. She and Tom found the house easily enough. The Littlegood place was a sizeable house in a clearing near the middle of Pook's Wood. No road led to it, however. The dirt track Mr Gloyn assumed was long tarmacked was still there, but it was strangely flat, which Polly thought was evidence no car drove down it. There would have been ruts. Instead the mud was packed flat.

Tom was excited. They crept close to the house. The clearing was uniform, the trees growing up to an imaginary circle drawn around the house. They'd approached the house at an oblique angle so could see a garden at the rear and through the encircling trees the cemetery marked on the map.

"Mr Gloyn said the cemetery was false," she whispered. "One of the ancestors built it. He called it a folly. No one's actually buried there. There are no actual graves."

Tom was rapt. He loved anything arcane and/or macabre, and the idea of a graveyard full of false headstones gripped his imagination.

"Someone lives here though. There's a bike."

Tom pointed to a contraption grey and dull by the front door. The bicycle was ancient. The brakes were not wires but a series of connecting metal rods, and the design was heavy and angular. On the front was a basket, the limp hair of dried onions hanging over the side. Polly pointed to where the wind was blowing the smoke from the chimney. The smoke was blown so flat it looked like a long grey cat was crawling down the wall.

"Weird there's so much wind here," she said.

"Weird they've got a fire in summer."

"The front door's open. It looks closed but it's a little bit open." She paused. "We should go."

"We're fine in the trees. I want to see the graves."

Polly was feeling anxious. A quality of the house unsettled her. Although she saw no one, the chimney smoke and the open door suggested someone might catch them. Moreover, the house itself seemed to regard them, and the open front door made her think of a person about to say something. The house was watching them, still and patient. Yet Tom was already some distance away, heading deeper into the woods but curving inward to connect with the graveyard.

Polly followed. She'd no choice because he was too far away to reach with a whisper and anything louder might betray them. The ground underfoot bellowed with every step, but no one came out. The house (and this felt, in the depths of Polly's alarm, a possibility) didn't turn to look over its shoulder to see where they were going. When they reached the graveyard, she was relieved to see the path that led to the back of the house was overgrown with tall grasses and fruit trees, rows of sweet peas lining the path. She and Tom were well hidden should anyone look out.

Tom pointed out low hedges. "It's a maze," he said.

It wasn't, but Polly could see it once was. The lines of the maze wound around the graves into a sunken area of land behind the house, right up to the edge of the trees. Tom was gleeful, and his feeling was infectious.

"This is the best," he whispered.

"I wonder if it was a *memento mori*," Polly said.

If the hedges that were intended to form the maze were high, every dead end would have had a grave in it. *Maybe that was the point*, she thought.

"Well grim," said Tom. He ran his fingers over one of the stones. "Look at how detailed they are."

Engraved were snakes, dancing figures, green men. One headstone had a graphic sex act centre stage. Tom laughed; Polly blushed. Other tombstones held little figures and hulked monsters, and scale was all over the place as giants and children occupied the same tableau. Lichen covered them all, which testified to their age, but all were rigidly upright, which backed up what Mr Gloyn had told her: that there were no graves, only headstones, and so the ground would not have sunk into the spaces beneath that once held human flesh. None of the stones had the expected information either, no names or dates. The closest resemblance was a gravestone reading *Mary Baker, dead at seventy-seven*. The numbers were spelt out.

Others had legends that might have been names – *Barguest* and *Selena* – while others held engravings more akin to captions on photographs: *Held Harvest, Pulling Cat-sparks, Low Wedding, Hunters' Hill*. Some were truly odd. *Teapot Plaque* read the strangest. The two shortest read *Thistles* and (her favourite) *A Hare*. The longest read—

> May your pockets be deep in dust,
> for each mote is a star, little one,

and your right pocket holds one world
and your left holds another.

"This is the best place I've ever been," whispered Tom.

At the centre of the maze had the hedges been tall was a larger grave. Polly understood then this *memento mori* held no escape. Death was even at the centre. Although the headstone was the largest, with a rectangle of dry grass in front of it big enough to have housed two bodies, the epitaph was short. *Where the Wasteland Ends.* Below this was engraved a spiral piebald with lichen. Tom was reaching for the letters when from behind the stone stepped a black dog.

The dog was about the size of a moor pony. The sight of it froze Polly to the spot. She'd never seen a dog that size before, and what was worse was that it was black, and not black in any usual sheepdog sense, but black in all particulars, even down to the whiskers and the eyebrows. The dog watched them; even the eyes were solid black. She felt the most complete fear, fear as if her blood had turned to gold, doubling her weight and killing all chance of escape.

"We should leave."

"I think it's okay," replied Tom. "It's not growling or anything." At his words the dog licked its lips, red tongue and deep red cave of a mouth. "Okay, we should leave," he said.

As they backed off the rectangle of grass in front of *Where the Wasteland Ends*, the black dog stepped onto the grave and lay long upon it, watching them as they hurried away.

That evening, her parents were out. Alan expected Tom to be at home in the evening, but Polly was used to staying in on her own. There was little risk in the country. The neighbour, old Mrs Tarr, kept her ear out for her. Mrs Tarr had the broadest accent and was eighty years old, remaining spry and interested in the world and her garden. Still spooked by the enormous dog, Polly decided she'd go to see her.

She found the old woman in the garden. It was dusk and she was gathering tomatoes and late rhubarb. "Can't beat stewed rhubarb," she said. "Cold stewed rhubarb on porridge of a morning. Nothing better."

Polly asked about the house in the woods. Mrs Tarr didn't speak for a while. Her mouth doubled in on itself. She had no teeth so her lips tended to the inward. She used her curved paring knife to cut tomato vines close to the stem.

"The son is a herbalist," she said at last. "Odd family. You never see them around. No end of money."

"I was out there. Me and Tom went walking. There was a black dog bigger than a moor pony."

Mrs Tarr shuffled her lips again. "I've seen that dog. When I was a little girl. Bigger than me it was."

"Probably a different dog," Polly put in.

"Black to its eyes and whiskers?" Polly nodded. "The same dog." Mrs Tarr straightened, a hand on her back. "You'll laugh at me but when I was a girl I was told about that dog by old Jane Weskit over at Tinford. She swore up and down a man pulled a pike the size of a yearling out of the River Linnet, and in its mouth was that dog as a pup, curled up happily asleep where the pike's tongue would be. You may laugh but she swore that up and down and I believed her." She fixed her little round glasses on Polly. "Don't go near that dog, Polly."

A quality of Mrs Tarr that Polly liked was that they were the same height. They regarded each other levelly.

"You said they had money. Don't they work?"

"You'll laugh even harder at this," Mrs Tarr said, even though Polly hadn't broken a grin. "I heard the grandfather found a coin on a post in the middle of Hundredwood. This was before the council murdered the trees. Just a wooden post in the ground. No one knew who put it there and it was on its tod. It wasn't part of a fence," she said, as if Polly had suggested it might be. "All on its own. So the grandfather takes the coin. Next day there's two coins. Next day four coins. The next day there's eight coins. The next day there is sixteen coins." Mrs Tarr held her tiny hook knife in front of her, looking like an owl in the dusk. "The next day there is thirty-two coins. And then the day after that, there is sixty-four coins—."

"They were doubling each time."

"And he never told anyone. If you tell, it stops. Years he went, every day, enough silver for a dozen lifetimes, and then one day he got so drunk he slept for a day and a half and missed a day. When he got there the post was bare."

Polly didn't believe this. She had a clear image of coins stacked in a pillar on top of the post. Even one hundred and twenty-eight would be tall, precarious. If doubling every day, she was fairly sure the rules of exponential growth would see the coin stack reach the moon in a surprisingly short space of time.

"Did you say he was a herbalist?"

Mrs Tarr gave an exaggerated shiver. "I've heard the women go out there. More than just the usual gripe water and folk remedies every-one around here knows. I've seen him at the markets. I bought some wildflower honey from him once. It wasn't to my taste." She paused. "I wouldn't go out there if I were you. The Littlegoods have always stood apart, if you know what I mean."

Polly didn't but when she told Tom the next day she saw the effect the words had on him. The whole of him flared open with excitement.

"It's rubbish," she told him. "Coins up to the moon and a fish with a dog in its mouth."

Tom told her of the dream he'd had in the night. He'd been there at the Littlegood house at dusk, yet this time the maze was not brown, woody scrub that barely reached the knee but tall hedges interspersed with the giant grass that lined the path to the graves. In his dream, he'd walked the maze, the way illuminated by the gold heads of sunflowers at the top of the grass. An eerie light threw his shadow around the corners of the maze, and in the darkness of his own shadow he heard distant music—

"I got so lost. Turning corner after corner to find a dead end and a grave." Polly laughed, and once Tom had heard what he'd said, he laughed also, less happily. "On the graves there was something alive, or new. Like on the grave called *A Hare* there was a hare, asleep. Ears like those crinkly scissors—."

"Pinking shears."

"Pinking shears. A trowel. A snake. Corncobs. Lots of food, like at harvest festival. Light all around." He paused. "Then I got to the centre. *Where the Wasteland Ends.* And that grave was open, steps leading down into the dark." He paused again and Polly thirsted for more, but he shook his head. "Then I woke up. My dad was coming up the stairs to go to bed."

"Probably his footsteps got into your dream."

He looked at her. "I can't imagine myself into his thoughts," he said. "He's not watching TV. He's not working or drinking. He's not doing anything. He just sits in pain. It was three in the morning."

Polly thought of what her father had said. *He's not in a place where deciding-to-be-better is a possibility. You're asking the man to turn the handle in a room that has no doors.*

Tom said, "I want to go out there again. Today."

Polly knew this before he spoke. She knew the house had taken hold of him on an imaginative and emotional level, and although the place – and the dog – scared her, she knew she felt a similar pull. Mrs Tarr was right: the Littlegood place stood apart.

She nodded, and while Tom popped indoors to tell his father he'd be back in the afternoon, Polly put together sandwiches and left a note for her parents. They'd stayed with friends the night before, and she knew they wouldn't even start toward home until midday. She slipped the note into the dial of the rotary telephone at the foot of the stairs then headed out to meet Tom at the gate. He was staring out at the grass where his mother had been trodden out of existence.

They walked fast, reaching the clearing before eleven, the sun high. The scene was similar: the bicycle, door ajar, smoke reluctant to let go of the wall. The house was lived in but no one seemed present. They walked entirely around the building, following a circle ten feet behind the tree line. *Like thieves*, Polly thought.

The trees were all silver birches. Some trick of their uniformity made her think a person was darting into their shadows whenever they passed a trunk. A small figure. After a while, she realised this was no illusion.

"Do you see a boy?" she asked.

"Yes. He's tiny. He's shorter than you."

"Thanks."

The child was also becoming bolder, wanting to be seen. He stayed out from the trees longer, unsmiling but clearly playing with them. Now she could see him for longer moments she realised he was about their age.

"I wonder if he's ill," she whispered. "I've never seen him at school. He doesn't look well."

"He looks grey."

Tom was right, yet the effect was deeper than his complexion. The boy didn't walk quite right, and although cricket-fast, there was an angularity to his movement. He moved like a robot until – with a click – he vanished like a flea.

"Look behind him," whispered Tom.

In the rear garden, just before the long grasses and sunflowers that hid the graveyard began, a woman in a summer dress was quartering the woods that circled the house, one hand shielding her eyes. She was young, mid-thirties, barefoot and lean. A phrase her grandmother used popped into Polly's head. *A no-knickers hippy.* She said this to Tom then wished she hadn't. She almost heard the blood in him begin to thud.

"Robin," the woman called.

The child was moving towards (they assumed) his mother's voice. There was a peculiar moment when he reached her, for he didn't speak but communicated clearly their presence in the trees. The woman looked up sharply, peering towards them.

"What if she sends the dog?" asked Polly.

"Her ears are wild," said Tom.

With her face turned to them, Polly saw at once what Tom meant. The woman's ears were lobeless, egg shaped, at right angles to her head, accentuated by her hair being tucked behind them. They gave her such a distinct look: unusual, adorable.

"She's coming towards us."

Later, after the descent into collapse she didn't know they were now entering, Polly wondered at the direction taken. At first it was simple to shuck off accountability like a summer frock, and to some extent this was true – Tom took the first step forward out of the trees without asking Polly first – yet she felt the same drawing towards the egg-eared woman. For Tom she suspected the draw was firstly lust, but a lust that hid a yearning for family and – though he'd likely never acknowledge it – a mother, but she also wondered if the quality of the image – silent boy and kindly mother – connected with the bereaved boy at a level beyond awareness or words. For her, however, once she'd fallen into step behind Tom, she was taking a conscious step out of the ordinary and into the strange, the new. It was a movement away from the staid world of her parents and towards the unknown dynamic of the Littlegood house.

"Hello," said the woman.

"We were here the other day," said Polly.

"Yes. Burgess told us."

Neither Polly nor Tom replied. It wasn't clear until later that the woman had meant the black dog. Standing side by side, Polly saw how distinct mother and child were: the mother tanned and golden, lit from within by an inner grace, and the boy sharp and grey, sullen and watchful. Polly introduced herself and, after a moment of silence, Tom.

"I'm Elfy," said the woman. "This is Robin."

The boy stared at Tom and did not speak. He paid Polly no mind whatsoever.

At first the visit was unsurprising. Elfy took them into the house and gave them a mini-tour as she got refreshments. The interior was cool and dark, with much clutter. Dusty couches and books were everywhere, an old plate filled with dead hand-rolled cigarettes on a low coffee table. A line of blue haze wavered above Polly's head, filled with motes, and she couldn't decide if it was smoke or simply the only light that managed to get through the closed curtains. The floor was wooden boards apart from a rug underneath the coffee table. Here and there were mugs of wildflowers picked from the garden.

Polly liked the room. In the spirit of the new, it was opposite to her experience. The couches were torn, one with an arm taken down to the wooden bones by a cat's claws, and books were on every available surface. There was no television. In the corner was a turntable and a stack of LPs. The front record in the stack was unknown to her. Virginia Astley, *From Gardens Where We Feel Secure*.

Elfy didn't show the upstairs, but they got to see into every part of the downstairs, even the cellar where jars of preserves and cordial sat dusty on rickety wooden shelves. "Peter made them," Elfy said, and it was unclear as to whether she meant the shelves or the preserves. She picked a bottle that had a sprig of white flowers at the bottom and took them up to the kitchen, again ramshackle, filled with dirty and chipped dishes, produce steeping in pickling liquid and bowls of muddy fruit and veg. *No end of wealth*, Mrs Tarr had said, but the kitchen looked more the kind of self-sufficiency that was driven by necessity.

In the corner sat a giant wood-burning stove that made the kitchen close. Polly began to sweat, and was thankful when they went back to the garden. Elfy pointed to the chairs. "Sit. I'll call Peter," she said.

Polly became nervous. Tom looked relaxed, eager. Under the motionless eyes of Robin, Tom whispered, "I love this place. They don't even have a TV."

"It is peaceful," she conceded.

"He's coming," Elfy said as she returned barefoot from the edge of the tall grass. She put one foot directly in front of the other as if she were walking a tightrope. Polly had never seen a woman walk like that, and it felt contradictory. Her gait looked both controlled and free.

"Visitors," said Peter Littlegood when he came out of the tall grass. He closed a small pruning knife with his thumb and put it in his shirt pocket. "We don't have many."

"We don't have any," said Elfy with a smile.

Peter was older than Elfy. She was mid-thirties, Polly guessed, whereas he was her father's age, mid forties, perhaps older. Elfy's hand found his when he sat. He was the type of fat that would be termed *cuddly* by those who loved him, and his whole self exuded well-being.

"I was very sorry to hear about your mother," he said to Tom once the introductions were done. "The shock will have altered you considerably."

Polly found this a strange phrasing, and the sentiment as expressed floored Tom for long minutes. It was only later that another curiosity occurred to Polly. Without knowing Tom's surname, in a house with no visible TV or newspapers, and as Mrs Tarr said no contact with the local community, she could not see how he knew Tom's mother was dead.

"We were out walking the other day," Polly said. "We stumbled on the graves."

"You stumbled on them?"

Polly faltered. "Yes. There was a black dog."

"She terrifies people," Elfy said, "but she's a sweety."

"The graves aren't graves, are they?"

Peter lowered his head and considered her. "Why do you say that?"

"All the stones are straight," Polly said after a short pause. She didn't know why she held back her knowledge of the plans and what Mr Gloyn had said. "They would have sagged. And, you know, the names—."

Slowly, and with a curious breathy *h* sound before he uttered the word, he asked, "Why?"

At first Polly didn't know what to say. "I thought *memento mori*," she replied after a moment, feeling a little hot at saying the Latin term out loud with an adult. A learnèd adult. Saying those two words was dangerous, the equivalent of showing puny human teeth to a tiger and hoping it wouldn't see it as a challenge—

Peter simply smiled. "I think so too. My grandfather made it. He never gave a reason. I keep meaning to get someone in to look at redoing the maze."

"You can do that yourself," said Elfy.

Polly thought the same thing. Mrs Tarr had said he was a herbalist. As if in answer to both, Peter replied, "I can make things grow, but I can't make them grow straight."

This first visit to the house in the woods passed quickly. There remained a faint air of awkwardness Polly couldn't identify and wondered if it was down to their having been effectively caught spying on the family. The next time they went, however, Tom and Polly slotted into the unit as if distaff cousins.

"Make yourself at home," Elfy said when they arrived the next day, flapping her dress by pulling out a button. "There's no air this time of year. Tom, you look strong—."

In retrospect it was natural they fell to an adult each. Although Polly didn't feel any form of sexual pull toward Tom, there was grit in her emotional shoe at how transparently Tom gravitated to Elfy. Tom's focus was the silent boy, Robin, but Polly knew Elfy was the draw: her golden light and cutesy way of standing that Polly read as intentionally *gauche*. She'd seen Elfy turn her toes in when Tom was near, making herself girlish, awkward. Elfy bit her bottom lip and looked away; she swung her arms from side to side; when sitting, she put her legs out straight and pulled her toes towards her to look at them. Elfy was aware of his awareness of her, and at times she knew Tom was aware of her awareness of his awareness. The only non-acknowledgement of awareness was when Polly teased him about it, then he denied he was doing anything beyond blowing out boyish energy with Robin. It didn't bother her, but it bothered her.

Robin never spoke. Not a single English word ever. "Elfy says there's nothing wrong with him," Tom told her. "He's just never spoken. He belongs to the woods."

"Is he—?" She paused. "All there?"

Tom shrugged. "I guess. He's a normal kid except he doesn't talk." He thought for a moment. "Or smile. But he doesn't seem unhappy. He likes playing French cricket. He loves that."

Polly knew this. Although they had fallen into two camps – Polly with Peter and Tom with (Elfy) Robin – the fall was slight. They were in view of each other at all times. While Tom and Robin played in the walled garden, Polly followed Peter into the wilder part of the clearing and sometimes beyond the treeline. The wilderness of wildflowers she'd seen was soon revealed as a garden plotted by an hysteric. What Polly thought of as random plants were all known to Peter, but there was no order to the planting. Polly loved to garden and had assembled a wide knowledge of plants, but a lot of the plants at the Littlegood house were unknown to her, and even plants she knew – foxglove, harebell, cornflower – seemed to have slipped category into medicine and not the shy beauties of the hedgerow as she'd imagined them. Flowers she'd thought delicate and unobtrusive Peter described in terms of muscularity and power. She'd heard him call a columbine *beefy*. He'd wander past blue charmers to seek out small brown nothings. She was sure at one point he called a fuchsia *a whore*.

Polly and Peter fell into a habit of call and response. She would name a flower or plant. He would give her the old names, some of which were so strange as to make her laugh. *Knitbone. Clown's mustard. Love-lies-bleeding. Witch moneybags. Sweet maudlin.*

"My neighbour says you're a herbalist," she said on their third visit.

"Mrs Tarr," he muttered.

Polly wondered again how a person who never seemed to leave his house or have any contact with the world beyond the clearing could have such a knowledge of the outside world.

"She said she bought wildflower honey from you."

He stared at her intently. "Probably. I used to have hives. They've gone now. I sold them to a woman in Hollow Thomas." He paused, looking into the distance. "I was sorry to let them go. I'm a bit flighty. I lose interest easily. Elfy is quite the eye roller when a new idea comes to me." He stared at her intently again, thumbnail peeling the outer skin from a muddy bulb. "*Herbalist* is as good a name as any," he said. He pointed to a plant. "What's that?"

"Yarrow," she replied.

"Yes. Also known as *Milfoil. Nosebleed. Soldier's-wound wort. Stanchgrass.* But for me it's a tiny green door into change." He made a gesture to encompass the garden, the trees. "Mostly they alter your world by their smell or their taste. But some will kill you, some make you sick, some make you feel—." He paused. "Combine them and a whole other world opens up. A healing world. A world of surprises. A world that opens up. Sometimes, a world into another world—

"You see plants, dozens, hundreds of varieties. When I see plants, I see a hilltop village from a distance, all the houses tiny, all of them with doors that hide what's within."

"You can cure people of things?"

"Yes." He was silent for a moment. An uncanny quality of the man was that he seemed to read minds. "Not grief," he said quietly. "The cure for grief grows in no earthly garden."

Polly was embarrassed he'd read her thoughts. From the apron with huge pockets he wore around his waist he pulled a handful of plants. This had become a test with them, one that reached deep into her love for knowledge. She loved to be quizzed. He opened his wide palm and asked her to name them, which she did for four. She didn't know their Latin names. Somehow the Latin names were too bookish.

The last plant he held she couldn't identify. "Give up," she said.

Peter didn't tell her. Usually he did, but this time he didn't. "What's *your* name for it?" he asked.

"That's what I said. I don't know."

He shook his head, and it almost seemed he was angry with her. "It has a name," he said, serious now. "In fact, it probably has a dozen. All of those names are its name, but they are separated out by place and time."

He moved the pole for the clothes line until the rope was by his eye. The plant, which was like a long green hare's ear that tapered into a white tuber, he popped over the washing line and placed it at varying points in front of him.

"The first humans would have had a name for it," he said. "We won't ever know that name." He moved the green ear further, further. "Norse, Old English, Irish, Gaelic, Anglo-Saxon, Norman, French. Possibly hundreds of names. *Buckram. Bear leek. Ramson,* from the Anglo-Saxon *hramsa.* Each of these names would've had another dozen known by local folk. Certainly the Norman word would have overlaid blunt old English names. Names of one syllable that sound like a pebble clicking on a stone. Then the Linnaean terms, common terms, terms fiercely local. Some of these plants even have medical designators now. Digitalis, for example—

"But something happened when this plant was given its Linnaean term. Science gave it its final name and the naming line stopped. No new names." He took the plant from the lowered washing line. "Our interaction with the world stopped dead. This plant has a book term. Mrs Tarr will surely have an old name for it, but everyone else——." He peered at her. "You, for instance, you go to the books. All of these you learn from books. Probably *The Observer's Book of the Garden* or something like that?"

Polly felt exposed, because it was in exactly these books she'd learned most of her terms. There it was: the jaws that she sensed in Peter Littlegood had finally snapped shut on her. Polly felt humiliated somehow, wanting to cry because she didn't know the things he knew and longing to be over where the tennis ball thocked on wood and people ran on grass. Yet when he looked at her again, his face changed.

"I am so sorry," he said. "I'm getting carried away with myself. And I'm travelling up my own bottom, as Elfy says." He smiled. "The first time I saw a VW Beetle as a child, I called it a *gaggy*. Its indicators were *tink-tonks*. For me that is the car's name. It will always be its name." He held the green ear out again. "My point is this plant can have any name you like. I regret the fact some Victorian tit dressed this robust plant in Latin, knotted its necktie and tied its corset laces for all time, but it doesn't mean it can't have any damn name you like. So I ask you again, Polly, what's its name?"

"*Hare bone*," she said then shook her head. "No. *Milk quill*. Its name is *milk quill*."

Peter's face opened up in delight. "That's wonderful," he said. "It's wild garlic, but I like your name better."

Although the man made her nervous, there was a hypnotic quality to him. He was pleasant, harmless. He was also absent in a way she liked. Everyone else in her life was intrusively present. However, when they were out in the garden, she always had the sense they were not alone. It was similar to the sense she had when they were in the woods before they first came to the Littlegood house. It was as if something in the corner of her eyes was watching her, and when she turned to look it was not there, but where her gaze had first been something else had now popped up.

"I keep thinking I'm seeing faces," she said to him, "but everything out there is flowers."

"I'm reminded of Friedrich Froebel. His idea of the *kindergarten*. The word literally means *the garden whose plants are children*." Peter looked at her, curious. "Our brains are conditioned to see faces," he said.

"I know."

"To the point the corners in an upside down triangle make a face."

"It's more than that. I get the sense sometimes there are other children crawling in the grass. Crouching in the grass." She paused. "Behind the trees."

"Like you and Tom were?"

She lowered her eyes. "I suppose," she said, and dropped the subject.

Peter was critical of science. He felt it was a bell jar. Science placed items in the world in isolation and cut off the air, but for him all was relational: every piece of the world was intimately interconnected with every other piece of the world. The bell jar of science was death. *Death-ful* was a word he used often, which Polly was sure he'd made up. Science reduced everything to items in a catalogue or scorn. *Knowledge fits in the catalogue or it's scorned*, he said, *Cat., or scorn*. Yet for him there was too much in the world that could not be explained away as illusory. To scorn it was the ultimate ignorance, and it was an ignorance of which science was guilty. Polly heard this talk as dangerous. School and school work was too present with her. She was entering the 'O' Level year in September. She was sure *catalogue* – in Peter's term – was right where she needed to be. Her mother would have bounced the man in a heartbeat, even though it was his own house.

Polly felt a pull towards him and what he was saying to her about the nature of existence. He was infectious in a way. The best evidence for this was that he told her the book name of the plants she couldn't identify, but now she couldn't recall those names at all. For her it was *fret-wort, giddy-bone, blue booby*. It took an effort of will for her to remember that *milk quill* was just wild garlic.

Those afternoons were magical. Partly it was summer – clouds, sun, the garden yelling in green glee from dawn to dusk, the occasional blithe squirrel – but it was also the convivial atmosphere of the garden in the clearing in the middle of Pook's Wood. At times Polly felt she was on a stage, some Greek amphitheatre and all around the trees watched their domestic play, yet it felt more than simply the trees, or the trees were not quite trees but two-way mirrors, or inside each trunk was a wooden room where a child might sit and stare outwards in secret at the world. Tom and Robin playing French cricket. Tom and Elfy talking low. Polly and Peter talking low. Peter mashing the ingredients he'd harvested into a paste with a button of his homemade soap. When he'd finished, he asked her to try it on her skin or lips. One might be cool. Another made her fingers buzz like Tiger Balm. One got into her nose when she smelled it – it stank – and made her sneeze at the time, but afterwards she got a whiff of it at times during the whole day and even smelt that scent in her dreams.

He asked, in that brusquely personal way he had, what she had tried for her permanently chapped lips, then sat talking to her about the dead hand of science as he mixed a salve in his mortar and pestle—

"We are a river," he said. "A human river, and we flow in the same channel as the animal river, the plant river. And there are still other rivers flowing in the same space, neither human nor animal nor plant—." He ground his base soap and stripped a vanilla pod into the mortar, working the whole together. "But the human river got dammed by expert knowledge. We are now stagnant. All the names are the same and evermore shall be so. Knowledge proceeds goose step towards the glorious scientific future. Deathful. Yet all around us the spirit river flows, the animal river flows, the nature river flows." He held up his pestle. "But we can find our way there if we open ourselves to those other rivers. They flow right beside us after all—."

He added honey and another substance he called *emulsified sativum*, together with a drop of silver oil Polly was sure he called *lurch*. He mixed again.

"I believe what science calls the human propensity to see faces and patterns scorns the truth. The truth is that there *are* faces and patterns that we shouldn't see. Consider the human felt sense of being looked at. Science explains it as the intuitive picking up of signals and blah blah blah. That's shit. You *are* being looked at all the time, by birds, rats, cats, little folk, dogs, beetles, trees, ants and daisies. And don't get me started on the chemical basis of love. Love is an expression of all the rivers running true. Ironic, considering Shakespeare's view. The course of true love, et cetera, et ceteranus. We are a river, and all other rivers run beside us, within reach, as long as we stop trying to control the flow."

He handed her the balm he had made. She took some on the end of her little finger and rubbed it into her lower lip. There was an acrid element to it, but on the whole it was okay. It wasn't until that evening that Polly realised the pain in her lips had gone, the lines flat and sealed. What she saw in her reflection every morning when she woke and smiled at the mirror – a tearing – lifted until the contents of the jar ran out. Her whole life she never found a better treatment, not until she and Peter met again.

The weather had been hot for days, unpleasantly so. People had been saying the weather was due to break. While Peter was in the kitchen decanting the balm into a small Kilner jar for her to take home, the sky darkened fast, seemingly coming in equally from all areas of the clearing.

"Here's that storm," Tom called.

They were sitting in a loose circle. Peter came over the grass with a pitcher of ice and elderflower cordial. In a moment the world changed. The light altered, sounds got louder and colours woke. She heard the ice click in the pitcher and Elfy breathe. The great black dog, who was rarely around, came close and she could hear it panting. Polly knew it was an effect of atmospheric or barometric pressure, ozone, a halting of wind and a sudden grey sink in temperature, but to her senses the sky itself seemed to simply relax and let go its burden.

The rain hammered down. The sun vanished as if fled, and the day grew dark. The first crack of thunder lifted her an inch off her seat, and somewhere close lightning stamped its white boot on the ground.

"Sit!" shouted Elfy. "Don't you dare move."

The woman was joyful, face to the clouds turning overhead. Tom, halfway running for shelter, sat, laughing as the sky shifted through the gears of a storm until the rain was battering down. The five of them sat, rigid as standing stones. They were soaked in seconds. Tom was laughing. Peter was blissfully staring at the sky, his hair dripping a line of water from his ponytail that looked like a stream of urine. Polly's skin came alive to the rain. Again, the sense was there of being on a stage. Her skin behaved as if the rain were applause thanking her for her performance in the play. Above her, the clouds were extraordinary, savage. They turned and turned and turned again. Grey kittens play fighting. But no, more violent than that. Grey and albino crocodiles rolling over and over in an effort to tear the weather apart. Thunder came again, lightning came again. The noise grew terrific, rain firing into the pitcher of elderflower water and off the roof. And *still* it rained: exuberant, giddy, glorious. Polly's hair was stuck to her face, her skin a river of wet.

"So," shouted Peter over the noise of the downpour, "how's school?"

When she looked at him, his face was light, mischievous. The question, so completely out of place, left her speechless, and she knew that was what he'd intended. His comment on the bookishness of the world of school in contrast to the glory of the storm. She put her arms out in the rain, pulled a face and shrugged as if to say, *How do I know?* Peter put his head back and roared.

The storm was ten minutes in when the hail came. "Hold!" screamed Elfy. "Hold fast!"

Given the season and the day, the hail was alien. *Where has such cold come from?* Polly thought. The fall was near painful but she loved to see the ice connect with such soft landing on the grass, gatherings of flung glass she could believe jewels.

Out of nowhere, she screamed. The scream took all of her lungs but this was nothing. She wanted to scream as though she was pulling the pockets of her body inside out to let the contents fall where they might, lost forever, and breathed in so deeply she felt her spine tense then again *let go*.

She let go.

On her second scream, Tom, Elfy and Peter joined her. They were all there together in a scream of release. And strangely, it frightened the storm clean away. The rain stopped, the clouds seemed to boil away, and moments later the sun returned.

"I'm cold," said Elfy. "I don't believe I'm saying this, but I'm actually bloody cold now."

In that moment, Polly realised the boy, Robin, hadn't screamed along with them. His emotional state, if emotional state there was, was diametrically opposite from the joy they all felt. In truth, he looked furious. Facing Tom, he opened his mouth, and without moving his lips to form the sounds that emanated, a chittering noise came out. It was the most disturbing act Polly had ever witnessed, as if a bickering of insects had exited his grey open hole.

"Robin," said Elfy.

Robin was intent on Tom, and Tom was bemused by the anger on the boy's face.

"Strange," said Peter.

Robin then turned to his mother and the inhuman sound again came out, almost angrier than the anger he'd expressed in a clatter of chitinous consonants at Tom. The boy and his voice were alien, adult, and Elfy turned white at the sound.

At once, Polly understood what the issue was. Elfy was not wearing a bra, and the rain had turned her dress not see-through exactly but clinging in a way that emphasised swell and a certain wet clarity in places, and in the definition of the nipples the adhesion was so clear she could see the goosebumps and a lengthy scar around the aureole.

Tom had been flattened by this apparition, and Polly felt a world of emotions towards him: annoyance, a measure of pity, a mean little nut of envy she didn't understand and, nearest to the surface, laughter – her friend looked like he'd stepped on a rake.

By this time Robin had left, his curious angular way of moving making his movement look mechanised as he vanished towards the false graves. Elfy, still white and visibly shocked, had risen uncertainly. Poor Tom's attention was nailed to her chest.

"Leave him," said Peter. "The storm got him. You know what they're like. He'll chatter out there until he's calm again. You *know* this, Elfy."

She nodded. "Maybe it was the lightning."

The whole afternoon had been rattled, yet Polly didn't believe either adult understood Robin's reaction had been to Tom's descent into orbit around Elfy's breasts.

"What was that?" she asked Tom as they walked home in the evaporating wet. "That sound made my hair stand on end."

"Don't," he replied. "It was like a science fiction film. Like an insect god inside him. Like it wasn't part of him."

"I wonder if he's an *idiot savant* or something."

"He's not an idiot," said Tom. "He just doesn't talk. Messing about with him—. I don't know. It's like he doesn't understand. I don't know. I can't explain it. It's like he only knows a few words in our language. He's clever. Fast. Really—. Present." Tom huffed, frustrated, then turned around to walk backward in front of her. "Know who he's like? Gaston. You remember Gaston?"

Polly knew who he meant exactly: a French exchange student the year before, delicate and bespectacled. Details filled in. Bowlcut hair, thin with a cartoon exactitude, but also an out-of-placeness more than simply difference of language and culture. One of the French teachers had been overheard calling him *pingouin*. Gaston had been strange even to his own kind.

"I remember Gaston," said Polly.

Tom turned to walk normally again. "That's the feeling I get with Robin," he said. "There's nothing wrong with him. He's just not fitting in here." He booted a stone. His still-wet jeans squeaked. "But why did I get his weird little cricket speech? That turned my hair white. He looked like he was going to kill me."

Polly answered this obliquely. She said, "Elfy wasn't wearing a bra."

Tom blushed hard. "I don't know what you're talking about. Christ, Polly, that's sexist. Why would you even mention that?"

Robin's insectoid reaction disturbed both their sleeps. They talked about this the next day on their way to Pook's Wood. They didn't realise it at the time, but it was the last time they would ever go to the house in the woods together—

Polly's dream was of a tapestry full of holes hanging in a grim damp old house. She could breathe it in her dream, so vivid she woke wheezing from the dust and mildew. In the dream, a hare was stitching into and out of the holes, forcing its ears through the tighter holes until they were through and shot upwards in a shudder. Polly couldn't see how the hare was able to do this on the vertical wall hanging until she saw the hare had four tiny human hands, by which it hung onto the tapestry.

"What was on the tapestry?" Tom asked.

Polly couldn't recall exactly. A hay wain, farm folk drunk in bales, pissing figures and revelry, all rendered unclear by the dirtiness of the dream-tapestry.

"I dreamed I was buried in one of those graves," Tom told her. "*A Hare*. That grave. I was scratching at the roof of the coffin, screaming. So scary. Then I felt someone tugging the back of my shirt. Like a little kid trying to get my attention. The *back* of my shirt. Tugging from below. Like there was a way out but it wasn't up but down." He paused. "And why should she wear a bra? It's her house, Polly."

Their individual days at the house were distinct. Tom had been helping clear one of the side buildings of the decades – perhaps centuries – of Littlegood tat that had accumulated. The building was to be a studio for Elfy. It being her need ensured his willing servitude. This was the entirety of his morning until Elfy called lunch and Robin came in from the woods.

In contrast, Polly's morning was spent with Peter. She'd expressed an interest in his homemade soap. It was a process he called *cold works*. He mixed the lye solution himself and put her on the solid oil process. Again, they entered a world of words savoury to their intellectual taste buds. *Sodium hydroxide, saponification, chromium green oxide, glycerin.* Peter didn't seem to mind these science words. They inhabited a world of pans, thermometers, cake moulds and whisks. He wielded a blender so lethal it looked like the propeller of a tiny motor boat.

As they worked, they chattered. He told her about a novel he was writing called *A Woodcutter*. She told him about school, the sense she had that what she was learning – what she was being taught – lay a distance

to the side of what was important, what was worth learning. Peter Littlegood gave a bark of laughter—

"Yes! The vital part cannot be measured so let us measure something
nearby and pretend *that* is meaningful."

"I don't understand."

"That the things that are worth measuring cannot be measured."

"The things worth learning cannot be taught?"

He pulled a face, which Polly read as criticism of the simplicity of
her question rather than its truth.

"Experience is the thing. What we're doing now—. I could give you
the recipe, but would you know by feel how to make soap? Trust me,
this has gone wrong so many times precisely because I have to *feel* when
it's right. When the soap thickens. When to leave it. Stand back." He
lowered the hand-held blender with its savage blade into the mixture
and, over the rumbles of its working, said, "So much of the world is
lost when being taught. It's top-down learning. To truly perceive the
world you need to clear out all expectations and prior learning, which
is the hardest thing to do. But at your age—." He shook his head hard.
"Scratch that. I'm not going to be that person—."

Polly liked him for that. She would have liked him to have gone on
speaking, but she liked him more because he didn't.

"Did you say *little folk* yesterday?" she asked. Peter didn't reply. "Yesterday, you said we were being looked at all the time and we don't know
it." Still he didn't reply. "Dogs and rats and birds. And I thought you
said *little folk*."

Littlegood was smiling now, ruefully. "I did. My little joke."

"Mrs Tarr said Burgess was born from the mouth of a pike and
your grandfather got rich from collecting coins from the woods." She
faltered. "That's what she said anyway."

"Mrs Tarr is country folk," Littlegood replied. "And perhaps that's
part of the same thing I was saying a moment ago. She sees the world
unadorned, without knowledge feeding in to close off explanation. To
narrow understanding into the thin channel permitted by modern life.
Which has the danger, I suppose, of sounding hugely patronising, as if

I'm saying she's thick. I don't mean that." Polly thought a judgement of *thick* was pretty fair. "Her understandings of the world are often dismissed as superstition. Superstition being explained away as uneducated people's descriptions of a world of phenomena they don't understand. But it's only a different way of seeing the world. And a more magical one—

"West of here there's a belief in the knockers, folk who live under the ground. It's thought they're the souls of the men lost in the mines, or perhaps the hidden children of Cain. You know the Bible?" Polly nodded thinking, *Why wouldn't I know the Bible?* "Others think of them as the souls of those drowned in Noah's flood, washed underground. A people who founded a republic of the lost there and whose openness to the possibilities of reality is far wider than ours. After all, Christianity was the first science. I don't mean in a good way. It was the first narrowing. The *huldufolk* were explained away as Eve hiding her dirty children from God when he was doing—. Oh, I don't know. The census. So she hid them from sight, like the bloody government with the unemployment figures.

"When I was a boy, my grandfather would tell me stories of the world that exists alongside our own. We cannot see it unless we are emptied of all expectations and beliefs. It's a brutal world that, even if we glimpse or suspect it, will vanish in the light of reason. Light burns it out of all existence.

"One thing he used to say was that if a wooden door has a knot missing, you should never look through the hole. If you do, you will see things invisible normally. Things otherwise unknown. I was a boy. Boys are lunatics. That's a Rebecca West reference, by the way. Their lunacy is immensely beautiful and valuable, but they're still lunatics. I tried on that door over there." He nodded to the broad wooden kitchen door. "I was on the other side of that precise door when I looked through. I found myself looking at Burgess, and as I watched I saw a tiny man clinging underneath sucking at her teats. This little man turned to look at me and spat a river of milk that tinkled when it hit the floor. The strangest thing was that my mother found a silver chain on the tiles that same day—

"Obviously, I was a child, and my grandfather liked to tell these old stories, and perhaps none of this ever happened. We all have these tales told of us that we think we remember, but in truth don't. But for my grandfather they were very real."

Peter looked wistful, distant for a moment. Polly looked at Burgess and thought, *How old is that dog?*

Her eyes turned to the door. She had noticed the hole in it before, noticed it because it was no longer there. A slice of cork from a wine bottle had been wedged in long before, as evidenced by the fact it had been painted the same bottle-green as the door. This fact more than anything made her skin restless. She could imagine Peter as a boy looking through and catching his life-altering visions of things otherwise unseen.

"I thought the little folk were supposed to be kind."

"No," he said, severe. "That's a Christianisation of them. That's the same road that made Easter all about chocolate eggs and bunny wabbits. That world—. If anything, it is a world where worth and value have no meaning or use. The worth of things, money, life itself. Almost quantum. Do you know anything about quantum dynamics?" Polly shook her head. "Doesn't matter. For us, an object can be worth something or nothing. It cannot be worth both something *and* nothing. For the little folk something is both valuable and worthless at exactly the same time. I'm thinking particle and wave here. And *worth* goes to the extremes for them. An object is nothing or it is fabulous treasure. It is the highest beauty and good or it is the lowest ugly and bad. Life at the extremes—." He paused. "Right, we need to concentrate now. This is a delicate bit."

When the soap was poured, they washed up. Polly liked the domesticity of it, the clearing of the sink and the gleaming implements once they were washed and air drying on the side.

"The worlds don't touch?" she asked.

"They touch. They touch all the time. In a way it's the same world and things cross from one side to the other constantly. Sometimes the dynamic is the same. It's as though the same tale is told twice. Dreary here, magical there." He nodded out the window, both of them ridiculous soaped up to the wrists washing up in the twin sinks. "What do you see?"

Tom was out there, stripped to the waist in the heat, pulling what looked like timber frames from one of the outbuildings.

"He's helping her."

"Why?"

Polly didn't answer. She didn't want to say, *Because he's a boy.* "She probably asked him to," she said at last. "Robin's not around."

Peter was silent for a moment as if wondering where exactly Robin was. "Consider this," he said. "Elfy's from a rich family. She went to Dermoût's. You know Dermoût's?" Polly did. It was a fabulously wealthy all-girls' school. "And Tom is the son of—?"

Polly shrugged. "I don't know. I think he works on a building site. Not a bricklayer but—."

"A contractor, foreman, something like that?" Polly nodded. "So, princess and servant. Elfy asks and her request is a command because of the difference between them. Status, power. Perhaps obligation? You are, after all, eating from our table and supping from our cellar. Yet did he have a choice? It's the way the world works. But could we view his servitude as a form of enchantment?" She laughed. He pushed his hands deep into the hot soapy water. "I can see enchantment." He paused. "You and he are not boyfriend and girlfriend?"

She blushed, hard. "No."

He looked at her directly. Side-by-side at the twin sinks, they were touching along their arms. "Okay. That's good. It pained me to think you were seeing that and had skin in the game."

"He does have a crush on her," she said.

"Oh, please," said Peter, "if she asked him to, he would suck the farts from her arsehole with a straw."

Polly giggled at the bluntness of this and couldn't stop. He began to laugh too—

"All I'm saying is that the world we see is more strange and complex than we are encouraged to believe. The chemicals in Tom's brain are a crush are love are enchantment are servitude to a queen. My grandfather believed that." He hesitated, looking deeply at her as if judging whether to further speak. "I have reason to believe it too, Polly."

He left this hanging, then said, "I need to take these to the cellar. Are you okay to finish up here?"

She nodded. "Can I take one of these soaps with me?"

"God, no. They take a month to cure. But these are ours. When they're ready, you can take as many as you want."

From the window, Polly saw Robin come in from the long grass. For a reason she couldn't quite define, the boy didn't look alone—

As she watched, Robin came up to Tom and started to dance. Tom looked uncertain, and she could sense his awkwardness. The dance was erotic, feminine. It made her feel hot, ashamed to be watching but unable to look away. In her peripheral vision, she saw Elfy hiding behind the door of what was to be her new studio. The woman had changed utterly. She was white with fear, hidden but watching this dance, now and then glancing to the trees behind, which is when Polly saw figures out there in the trees. Shadows. Faces peeking out with sharp features. But if she looked directly at one face, it became a bit of the tree. It was a face when she wasn't looking directly at it, but when she did look directly at it, it could have been something else. The experience was dislocating. She knew nothing was out there, and yet—

Robin danced up to Tom. There was an erotic quality in the dance, the small, grey boy grotesquely inadequate to the task of seduction, as curdling a sight as seeing her dad body pop. His movements were slow and snakish. He rolled his shoulders, moving towards Tom with all that *attention* from the woods behind.

Tom stood awkward and silent, sun beating down, dirty and dusty and having no clue how to react when Robin took his hand, slid his thumb gently to the elbow, then lifted his thumb to reveal what looked like a cat's elbow claw but of white bone projecting, which Robin dragged back down to Tom's hand, opening him from elbow crook to wrist. Blood was suddenly everywhere.

Polly backed into the corner by the door as Tom was brought in. The kitchen was changed in an instant, Tom at the sink dripping into the water, his entire forearm pulsing with blood. Peter left and returned with a fistful of medical gear so old she could see the yellowing on the packages.

Elfy was the surprise. She seemed two women, one white and terrified, muttering, *I'm so sorry*, yet her hands belonged to a creature with the brisk and ruthless efficiency of a school nurse. When she had rinsed Tom's arm elbow to hand, she ran her thumb over the wound, lifting the cut edge like an envelope whose gum has given slightly and the edge lifted. The cut was nine inches long, but the blood had slowed. Polly felt as if the whole of her innards would come out at the sight of that lifted flap of cut skin.

"It's not deep," Elfy said. She pressed gauze along the cut and told Peter to hold it as she bandaged. "I don't think it'll need stitches. It didn't go deep. Sort of sideways."

"Like he was trying to cut the skin off?"

"Peter!"

Tom caught Polly's eye. His arm against the woman's bloody dress looked delighted. The idea an arm could look delighted made no sense at all, but to Polly at the time it made absolute sense. The whole of Tom looked delighted. He wasn't frightened; he was excited, alive. She almost thought triumphant, and how oddly like a family unit they were: attentive and concerned father and a mother like a battlefield angel tending the wounds of the fallen.

"Where's Robin?" asked Peter quietly.

"He ran to the woods."

Polly's eyes flickered between the adults. They were smiling now but she intuited worlds of panic underneath. Elfy took them both to the living room, taking care to plump cushions conspicuously for Tom before he sat. With a sharp annoyance Polly saw that he loved this attention, and when Elfy left she said so. "You're loving this."

He grinned at her. "It didn't hurt. I didn't even know it was happening. Peter was right. He cut sideways. Like he was peeling an apple."

"Don't." She paused, lower lip in her teeth. "We should go," she said. She was right. They should have gone.

Through the window she saw Peter and Elfy talking urgently outside the house. An argument. *We can't call them*, was the only distinct thing she heard from Peter, high pitched and frantic.

Polly turned to Tom. "Was it part of him?"

Tom nodded. "It was like a bone sticking out of his thumb. About halfway down his thumb like cats have. A jabby bone. I thought he was stroking my arm with this thumb but the sharp bone was——." Tom stopped and pressed his arm. "It doesn't hurt at all."

Peter and Elfy had moved further from the house. Elfy was talking now, Peter with his hands at the small of his back staring into the woods.

"He was going for my veins. My arteries," Tom said. "It was only that I twisted away——."

The door to the living room creaked open. In the doorway stood Robin holding a tray. On his face was a sickening smile, as if it had been assembled using tacks inside his mouth to pin the muscles in place.

"Hello, Robin," said Tom.

The tray held cups and a teapot. No milk. Robin came closer. That smile made Polly want to run screaming, but she understood this was an apology. The boy's teeth were as grey as his skin, a gap between each as though his teeth were pegs in a cribbage board.

"Hello, Robin," she said.

He pushed the tray towards her. At the lip was a shaped length of paper, which Polly realised was the torn-open paper casing of the bandage, so old it had retained its balled shape at the end. On the inner helix of the paper wrapper was written—

eyuwoodlyksumtee?

Polly showed it to Tom. The horrific grin turned from one to the other of them.

"*You'd like some tea*," he said. "Jesus, the spelling."

Polly put her thumb under the question mark on the paper. "*Would you like some tea?*" she corrected. She nodded. "Yes, Robin. We would like some tea."

The grin nailed onto his face didn't change. *A shark*, she thought, *he looks like a human shark.*

The boy poured tea. They each took their cups. Tom sipped. "This isn't tea."

"It's herbal tea," she replied.

In the cup were leaves. The liquid was opaque and thicker than normal tea, slightly sweet. The hub of a small flower turned idly at the base of the cup.

"It's nice," she said.

It was. The tea had a breathy sweetness and a creosoty bite that was not far distant from dandelion and burdock. For some reason it cleared her nose at the same time as settling a wheeze in her throat, and for a moment she wondered if she were allergic to one of the ingredients. Above all, the tea tasted natural and clean; it tasted as if its intent were good.

"Robin, it's OK. You can stop smiling."

"Yes, it's okay, Robin," echoed Tom.

The boy didn't stop smiling, but he clearly read their words as absolution for he turned that crime of a grin to the kitchen and left.

At first, Polly experienced the change as a temperature rise. Tom said as much himself. She was fifteen, Tom was sixteen. Neither of them had even been drunk before. The experience was new and therefore unrecognised. Polly wondered if it was a summer flu. She was aware of Tom next to her staring at the weave of his bandage.

"This is snow," he said.

When the man and woman came through the door, she didn't recognise them, and it seemed to her as though they'd been painted in place. The man had a hairy ponytail; the woman was as eary as trophy handles. They were not natural. In fact the only natural beings were the trees and grass outside the house and the plants inside the house. And, curiously, her and Tom. The hairy man and the eary woman were like oil paintings, hard paste out of which the appearance of *things* had been formed—

The same was true of the walls, the doors, and oddly she felt the door-timber's pain. The wood had been wounded, tortured, used, as had – it was everywhere! – clay and stone and iron. The room was filled with *things* she couldn't recognise and that were violent somehow. The woman's bloody dress. The man's dirty shirt, sleeves rolled stranglingly up his arms. The woman's feet were raw on the murdered wood, and the man wore the torn-up skin of a beast into which needles had been punch-sunk, sockets threaded with string, maybe where an eye had been ripped from the corpse's skin. Below the strings of his feet creatures was a form of of flat pith. The feet creatures' lips were choking on his ankle bones, mouths forced open to house their girth. Her bloody dress was a horror of cottonskin torn—

The man said, "We can't have the police here. We want to say how sorry we are this happened. And hope—."

The woman spoke. "We hope we can all draw a line under this. And if you could not tell your parents—."

"It would mean a lot. To us."

"To Robin. We can't have him taken away."

There was a lengthy silence.

"You should wear a bra," said Polly at last. "Everyone can see your tits. Tom can see your tits."

"They are there," Tom confirmed.

The word *tits* was like a dropped pot in the room. The eary woman crossed her arms. "Okay," she said, hesitant.

"Your teats," said Polly. "Your zaps."

"This isn't—. Peter?"

"You should have put on an over-the-shoulder-boulder-holder for them bazookas."

"This isn't like you, Polly," the hairy man said quietly.

"Your knockers. Your shirt potatoes." Polly frowned. "Your tatas."

Polly said this last as if she were saying goodbye to someone. Tom was howling with laughter. She pointed at the woman sternly. "Your dagnabbits," she said.

"What's wrong with them?"

"Nothing. You have lovely breasts."

"No. *Jesus*, Peter. What's wrong with *them*?"

The man went to the cups, holding the accompanying note up so the woman could read it. "He made them tea," he said. He put his nose in the violated clay. "He made them the tea."

"Your breasts," said Polly.

"We can't send them home."

"We've no choice."

"But if they get lost?"

The man thought for a moment. Polly heard Tom's laughter as water running over rocks, all knees and giggles. "One of us will have to walk them to where they can see their houses. Hell, walk them home."

"And the state of them? When they get there?"

"What else do we have? What other options do we have now, Elfy?"

The woman walked them into the woods. Polly was blinded by the hot sun. It was still high in the sky, the heat a rocket even under the leaves. Tom, still laughing, was held by the woman because he kept trying to run. She had a finger worked through a belt loop at the back of his jeans. Halfway into the woods, she stopped and wound Polly's finger in that belt loop until her finger was throttled.

"See? That's the path," the eary woman said, smelling of hot milk and copper. "Can you see the houses?"

Polly turned. There were houses. "I *can* see the houses."

The woman paused. "Do you recognise the houses?"

Polly turned back. "I *do* recognise the houses."

"You should go to sleep when you get home. You should both go to sleep when you get home."

"We should!" said Polly, delighted. "We should do that!"

The woman turned Polly's finger a last time in Tom's belt until it bulbed red. "Don't let him run off, Polly." Polly bit her lip. "Don't tell about Robin. Please don't tell."

Night had fallen by the time they reached the next tree, and the woods were thick with silver moonlight. Polly saw Tom in the distance, chin on a birch looking up the trunk in wonder. She was certain and then not certain that only a second before the sun had been high in the sky, and there was a dim memory she was heading for houses, but now they were in the centre of birch woods and the darkness was alive with traffic. Foxes were in the undergrowth, badgers, here and there the slitherings of glow worms and snakes, who, even though they were snakes, were English, quite apologetic and at heart good. Hares and voles and mice and rats were busy at the level of the ground. Polly felt other creatures were walking in the trees, or just behind the first row of trees, like pilgrims highstepping over the scrub carrying packs and bundles and instruments, yet she had no actual sight of any of these beings, only the sense of muttered movement and distant song.

The night was dark. She was about to join Tom when she realised he was not alone. A woman was there, a very different woman from the eary woman, and Tom was explaining he was looking at the insect tribes—

"The edges of their territories glow," he said, "and you can tell where the birds are because it's where the insects are not."

"The insects in these woods are known for being circumspect," said the woman.

The way she pronounced *circumspect* – so quiet and unlikely a word – was so perfect that Tom took his chin off the trunk and stared at her. The woman opened a drawer in the tree and took out a bottle of yellow liquid, pouring them both a cup, which Tom drank.

The woman was tall, sharp featured, and unusually dressed in a finely tailored coal-black suit with wooden buttons. She stood with one hip cocked, which made the trouser pocket on that side open like a cat's ear for Polly to see the lining was a deep silken red. The sharp woman's collar was open at the neck, and at her throat was a small bone on a leather thong. This was all Polly saw because the woman turned, hiding Tom, and the black cloth of the suit against the night made everything black, which was the point Polly realised they had both vanished from sight.

The music was audible now but the travelling people were still just shadows somewhere out there in the trees. "Tom," she called. "Tom, where have you gone?"

It was impossible they should be in the middle of a dark wood when the houses had been *right there*, but she was lost, alone, and the bustle of traffic out in the trees began slowly fading to silence. There was no clue as to the best direction to go.

Polly turned on the spot to find a gentleman leaning on the tree behind her, his fingers pulling at the bone he wore around his neck.

"The woods are mischievous tonight," he said. "I doubt you've the ear for it, but they've been playing a merry game with you. Would you permit me to lead you out?"

Polly didn't know what to say. Neither response represented her feelings on the matter, but she knew she didn't want to be alone in the silent wood so she nodded.

The man walked in the exact opposite direction to the one Tom and the strange woman had gone. "Come," he said.

"But shouldn't we go that way?"

The gentleman paused. "That's the way we're going," he said, "we're just taking this path."

He stepped in front of her and – so strange to say – while she was in his shadow he stepped forward and she had the sense she had been standing on a flat conveyor belt as she was taken through a dark doorway. It took less than a second, and the next thing she knew it was pitch dark and they were walking side by side through darker woods.

The path was winding and never very wide. The way was also hilly, which was foreign to her as the land around Cubton was fairly flat. The dark was cut with candles sunk into wooden cups on the trees, set low, about knee height. They offered little illumination but enough to light the way miles ahead. None of the candles was the same shape and all were at a different rate of burn. The gentleman did not talk save to excuse himself when the path got too narrow and their arms touched. Nor was he particularly visible. With the candles so low and him so tall, the light barely reached his neck. The most he shared with her was a snack he wrestled out from his red pocket.

"Would you like a bee?" he said, making the brown paper bag rustle. She took one. "Go on," he said, "take a handful."

Polly did so. The bees were nothing in her hand, light as popcorn. Shyly, from the corner of her eye, she looked to see what the gentleman was doing; how he was eating them. He cracked the bees open like a pistachio with a thick silver thumbnail. The motion was smooth. All he did was twist with this butter-knife thumbnail and the bee's centre came out. He flung the crisp shell into the trees. Polly copied him. It was hard at first, but soon she found a seam in the guts of the bee and with a crack the black-and-yellow shell disgorged a golden bean that she put in her mouth.

"It tastes like honey," she said.

"Well, yes," replied the gentleman.

They walked for a long time, the way so twisting Polly could not tell where they were going or how far they had come. Now and then the gentleman would point to something in the woods: an upright stone ring, a standing stone, a tree tied in a knot, a tor grey on a hill but for a blade of gold light that looked like a door slightly ajar leading to a room lit by candlelight just beyond.

"David Pease crawled through that," he said of the stone ring. "He could read when people were near death ever after. They sweated a clock out for their last twelve days on earth but only he could see the wet numbers lift off and fall. He never waited out the numbers on his own wet clock though," the gentleman said. "He slit his throat at eleven."

The standing stone was a poor mother who'd wandered blind into the woods; the tor belonged to a woman called Leanne Silver, and the rooms within were a still for a lethal brown gin. Polly asked about the tree tied in a knot. The gentleman glanced over. "A tale of great criminality," he said—

"There were two thieves, one fat, one thin sat in the snug of an inn. Each had drunk the best part of a bottle of plum wine. They were both old and poor, and neither had stored metal enough to buy them comfort in the lees of their lives, and they bitterly moaned about the men who'd fooled them out of their worth, the women who'd stolen their lust. A fat black tabby at the hearth looked up at them now and then, gave them a stare, huffed, yawned.

"Fat pulled a cake wrapped in paper from the back of his coat. It was bent, but sticky and fresh. *How low we've sunk*, he said. *My latest theft is a courgette cake stolen from that house by the hill. That reminds me, though,* he added, *of a queer sight when I was on the rob.*

"Fat told Thin as they ate the cake that he'd been tiptoe through the pantry when he heard footsteps on the floor above. Cursing his luck at finding the house inhabited, he turned to leave, fingers alighting only on the cake for his trouble. As he was creeping out, he caught sight of twenty cats looking in through the window above the sink. Fat only had one peek at the sink as he left, but the sight was fixed in his memory. In the sink was a blue box and beside it a lid. The box was fine-hewn and -fixed with turned handles and by the side six turned wooden screws waiting to secure the lid to the box. *And inside the box,* said Fat, *was a dead cat, chin up, front paws down by her sides like she'd keeled over flat backwards. She'd a smile on her face like she'd drowned in the top of the cream, and she was stone black apart from a brown ring, like a wood toggle had been slipped down her tail. I mean, why so much fuss for a cat?*

"Thin shook his arm and pointed to the fat tabby. *Now why,* he asked, *does that cat look so astonished?*

"Fat and Thin both looked at hearth cat, who was staring at them with great interest and surprise.

"*You have just described Molly Dixon,* said the cat, *and if Molly Dixon's dead, that means I'm king of the cats!*

"The tabby turned and dashed up the chimney.

"The two thieves had had a lifetime of spotting the value in a thing (and then selling it on too cheaply when they were drunk) and the thought of what a talking cat might fetch put fire in their heels. They ran into the street and watched the tabby bounce over the rooftops, following it at street level. At the edge of the village, it fled up the wise tree that stood in the middle of Hundredwood.

"Old as they were, Fat and Thin climbed the tree, high into the branches. Halfway up that tree is a natural chair where a child might sit and look over the town, but that evening Thin put his hand on it to find empty space. The two thieves pulled themselves up and looked over the lip of the hole. The trunk was hollow all the way down. A spiral staircase ran down the centre, and around the staircase was a bedroom with a sleeping box, a cradle, a night-larder, cupboards, a short bed for easement. Velvet wallpaper in the design of interlocked birds lined the inside of the trunk. Further down the trunk hollow, Fat and Thin saw another circular floor with a set of tavern games, then another floor, and another, all the way down into the earth.

"*So tiny*, said Fat, *like a house for poppets.*

"At the bottom of the shaft, they saw a tail vanishing around the spiral staircase. Thin seized the end banisters and pulled the spiral staircase out as if it were the spine from a fish. Head first he entered the trunk, bracing his hands on each floor as he let himself down the shaft. His shoulders scraped off chairs and desks, shattering them to splinters, but he didn't care. He had to get that cat.

"As he went down, he saw that knotholes on the outside of the trunk were windows from the inside, and each looked out at the dark village in the distance. When he passed ground level, he came to another window and expected it would look out into darkness, or have soil spilling in. Instead, he saw a clean summer lawn, grass as pertly green as if rain had just fallen. The sky was a blue out of nature. In the centre of the lawn were a thousand cats, their backs to him, staring up at the talking black tabby, who was now drinking a yard of ale and wearing a thirteen-point crown, on each tine of which was impaled a mouse. *King of cats!* called the worshipful throng when the ale was drunk.

"Thin couldn't believe what he was seeing. *The blood is in my head*, he thought, *I've been upside down too long.*

"The cats rushed by him, over his body and down further into the hole. He couldn't get a grip on one, but somehow each cat pressed two or three pieces of gold into his hands or pockets. His head was hot with blood now, but the gold was real, more wealth than he'd ever earned (or stolen) in his life, each coin heavy with a greenish patina to the metal.

"To give himself space to right himself, he'd to destroy four floors of the trunk. In the process he lost about half the gold from his pockets. He swore, battered the inside of the trunk, but a quick feel convinced him he was still the richest man he knew, and anyway, he thought, it was Fat's share of the booty that had fallen out.

"Slowly, he began to climb back up the trunk, but he began to notice something strange. Every time he pulled himself up a floor of the trunk, the gold in his pockets grew heavy and the trunk taller. To lighten himself, he'd no choice but to drop the gold coins piece by piece; however, for each bit he let fall, the remaining pieces seemed to adopt that weight as their own. His tears flowed, his muscles shrieked, but he could not climb out with the gold, and eventually he'd lost every last piece.

"Almost at once, he came to Fat, who'd become wedged in the trunk. This didn't surprise Thin. What did surprise him was that Fat had aged horribly fast and was now dead, a dusty skeleton suspended from where his pelvic bones had caught on one of the floors above. His hair was three feet long, his nails curled into screws, his bones yellow. The man looked to have been a hundred and fifty years old when he died.

"*Fat*, Thin said. *Oh, Fat.*

"He wailed, he moaned, he begged the cats to dash up the trunk to help him, but there was no sound from anywhere. At last he came to the realisation that his only escape was through Fat.

"Bone by bone, he took the skeleton of his friend apart and passed the pieces down the hole, dropping each one where it disappeared without a sound. The skeleton still had gristle at the knuckle bones, so Thin had to twist back and forth until each came free. Each gristle-creak as he twisted sounded like a cat's gleeful miaow. Jaw, spine-bones, ribs all went down the shaft bit by bit until he managed to unhook the pelvis and pushed the bottom half of his friend down the hole.

"And there's the end of the tale," said the gentleman. "Thin planted a sapling above his grave and the tree grew into that shape."

The hill grew steep, the path cobbled. Polly and the gentleman passed cottages the size of dolls' houses, weavers on the front porch, and a brewery that belched smells that recalled her father's under-stair gin cupboard. Her legs grew weary, and she began to fall behind.

"Where are we going?"

"You wanted to go home. I'm escorting you home."

From one moment to the next, they stepped out of the trees into the wasteland that was Murdered Wood. The change happened so fast.

There was forest and then there were the felled trees. All was familiar now, and although turned round, she knew the way home. Her head felt clear, clearer now that she saw Tom in the middle of the wasteland, the great black dog standing beside him. Yet when she called to Tom, he turned to her and replied, "Burgess?"

The significance of this statement didn't strike Polly. She ran toward her friend. With all the trees felled, the earth of Murdered Wood was treacherous, the soil having pulled back from the roots like flesh from the fingernails and hair of the dead. She tripped a number of times, once going flying. The wood in the moonlight looked like the surface of the moon, but a moon that instead of craters was dotted with vast wooden discs, or, as she now realised when she saw Tom twisting into the ground, missile silos.

"Tom," she called again, and he looked at her, giving her a wave before he vanished below the surface.

Where the tree had been cut level with the ground, instead of the stone trunk with its rings and scars was a helical staircase going straight down into the ground. Light blazed down there, spilling in from rooms off to the side of the stairs. Polly looked back to where she'd left the gentleman, but there was no sign of him. As such a sight had been the focus of his tale, she felt immense dread. There was no other interpretation than that the tale was a warning, yet Tom was a long way down now, so much so that when he looked up to see if she was following, it took her a moment to recognise him. With her head over the hole, she was in a chimney of music, laughter and speech she couldn't quite make out. She looked once around her and then, helpless to do anything else, followed Tom in.

The shaft was not human made. It rooted off as a tree would, the steps of the staircase uneven, finding a home wherever was nearest to a root. This meant some risers were high, giving her ankle a jolt when she landed, and some steps were shallow, which made her titter down the steps on tiptoe. The further she descended, the wider the staircase's gyre. When she looked up, the circle of the night sky was as small as a coin and the stairs of her descent formed a spiral.

Strangest of all was that rooms lay off the main stairs. This slowed Polly's descent as she had to look at what was within. There were rooms of gold light filled with candles and what looked like cradles of golden babies. Another where all was made of tight woven feathers, the chairs with up-hooked arms like an owl descending, the hearth made of pure white feathers. A tiny man on a chair upholstered with peacock tail feathers lifted his cup of tea to salute her as she passed.

A room was filled with five burly women at the bellows and hammers forging small daggers. A girl tugged a length of soft material from a series of puckered holes in the wall, which Polly soon realised were men's bellybuttons, only bellies visible as the rest of the person was walled up, and this bellybutton felt was worked into bright little knives.

There was no fit to the rooms. They could not all exist in the same place. A bedroom where two young men performed an extraordinarily intimate act on an old woman wearing an armoured chestplate gave way to a room packed with joyous dancers, and then to a room where a man whose skin was half white and half red was suspended upside down, screaming. Some rooms opened into other forests, another onto a silver road through a wood, the path lit with the lights that hung over pool tables, the white rectangles diminishing in glow like inverted road markings. A school room where children were grouped in fours around an amputated foot, which they were learning to tickle, and the dead feet responded as Polly would have expected while a woman with the head of an eagle marked the children's efforts.

Lower, lower—

Next was a room where a line of humans, mostly women, were suspended with their heads arched and their knees bound to their chest. Polly saw a hook dangling from their bottoms to which dirty sheets were attached before being tugged agonisingly through their bodies and out of their mouths, where they came out clean, ready to be ironed by the snakes.

She suspected the roots never ended and the stairs went on forever. When it struck her that the way up would be harder than the way down, she stopped. On one side of her was a room leading into a secret garden with high walls, a girl in a blue dress picking the discreetly coloured wild-flowers of an English meadow. She was followed by a gang of teen boys whose fingers had been stitched together in a cradle, their arms bound to their upper bellies. Polly could see where twine had been punched into their rib cage to tie their arm bones tight behind their ribs. Into this shallow soil-filled shelf, the girl dipped her little finger and planted a plucked shoot.

Behind Polly was a pool in a cavern, blue-lit and glinting with quartz. A woman bathed there, naked, two furry babies attached to her chest like pilot fish, her tail curved like a dolphin's.

To her right a cat, casual as a newsagent in a kiosk, was polishing the forearms of rodents, bones only, laying them finely in a cutlery case: shrews for dessert, mice for starters, rats for main course.

Ahead of her, she saw Tom in a meadow. He'd clearly tired at the same time at her. Tom turned to her. He put his finger over his lips and pointed—

As she walked towards him in the heat of the underground day, through the glorious grass and the hot sun, he moved to one side to reveal an enormous chest with a hundred drawers in it, all open. The chest looked like something in an old-fashioned chemist's, but instead of dried herbs and potions in the drawers there were cats, sleeping, bodies rising as they snored like bread in baking tins.

Polly tugged at Tom to warn him that they must leave, this place wasn't safe, but then, on top of the huge chest, she saw a boy about their age lying on his side. The boy was dressed in a green suit, a silver pocket watch in his waistcoat pocket. He was sleeping, his face fallen towards them. The recognition Polly felt in her bones and water. It was Peter Littlegood's face, so similar it was uncanny, except for the ears, which were lobeless, egg shaped, at right angles to his head.

"Is that—?"

As soon as she spoke every cat awoke. From behind her she heard a splash and a girl scream.

Tom grabbed her and whispered, "Don't speak. They don't speak to us. I don't think they see as at all. But they can hear us."

Polly kept silent. Tom was right. Although alert and standing on the lips of their respective drawers, none of the cats were looking at them. They searched black-eyed and fat-tailed before they fled, the backfoot push slamming all drawers perfectly shut with a sound like a string of firecrackers.

The sound woke the golden-haired boy. He opened his eyes and saw them. "Hello," he said.

Polly and Tom froze. From a stairwell in the grass a woman climbed, a golden basin in her hands. The basin was filled with honey.

"Who do you talk to?" she asked. The boy gestured. "There's no one there. Let me wash your hair."

Obediently, the boy let his yellow hair fall over the edge of the dresser, shielding his eyes from the sun with his hands. The woman was enormous, simply dressed in a frock of rough tweed, sharp-featured and hulking. She stroked the boy's hair into the golden basin full of honey, her hands large.

"There's a boy and a girl standing right there. The boy is tall and the girl is tiny."

The woman stopped what she was doing and said, "You see a boy and a girl?"

"I do. They are both pretty. If they could be unclothed and washed and brought to me——."

"I cannot see them. Point them out to me and I will blind them."

She smiled, teeth like white triangles, shark teeth against the grey innards of her mouth. She placed a basin on the ground, honey from the boy's wet hair spooling back into the bowl thickly as she approached.

"Oh, Mossycoat, you can't leave a job half done," the boy complained. "Half done is ill done. Isn't that what you always say? Half done is ill done."

Mossycoat was getting close now. From her pinny pocket she'd taken a pinch of petals that she was now grinding to a powder in her palm with a thumb that only now did Polly realise was the size of a courgette.

"Point them out to me," she said. She crept toward them. "Tell me when I'm getting close."

Tom was the first to run. He almost toppled Polly in his urge to drag her along with him. They whirled up the stairs, Tom ahead of her with his longer legs. Behind, the giant woman called Mossycoat insisted others help her—

"They know my name!" she hissed.

Up they fled. From all around came the sound of music, a column of song rising upwards. The occupants of the rooms came to the doorways and joined in the signing of the saddest song. The sorrow in the song got Polly in her knees. It felled her, literally. She sat on a step anchored to a rising tree root with wooden nails and could not move for the sadness that overwhelmed her.

Tom, on the other side of the helical stairs and a little higher than her, was similarly affected. The singers were above, below, around them, behind them, the song low and slow, not English but full of insects and mournful vowel sounds and so extraordinarily melodious it seem to fill up her lungs. Underneath the song of great sorrow was a single low drone note that Polly slowly realised was coming from the rope ascending from the depths to the surface. The rope hung in the centre of the shaft, humming like a chthonic bass guitar string in a note that affected her bones.

She yearned to speak, to draw Tom's attention to the rope, but she knew speaking would betray her position, and though the giant woman had stopped chasing, Polly could feel her beady attention below, palm filled with powder intended for her eyes.

Tom had seen what she'd seen, for he pointed below—

The long rope was pulling a coffin up from the depths. As it passed each level, the song of great sorrow swelled as the voices there lifted in volume. As the coffin approached her level, Polly saw there was a window sunk into the polished wood. The coffin was hauled up longways, and that window was facing Polly as it twisted past her. She could see clearly the face through the square of glass, pale in the coffin but lit from within by candlelight. The rate of twist was such that the window was still facing away when it passed Tom. She was so pleased that he did not see that the body in the coffin was his own.

The song of great sorrow had swelled at their level, rising with the coffin. Below the level of song the singers had fallen silent, which was when she heard a mess of footsteps and Mossycoat was upon her—

No resistance was possible. Polly was thrown into the nearest root-room. Held down by children, Mossycoat's monstrous face sailed into place above her—

"You can see me," said the woman. "I can't see you, but you can see me. Can you see me with both eyes?"

Polly later had no idea why she said what she said, but she replied, *No*. Split open with fear, she told Mossycoat she could only see her with her left eye. When her huge thumb had felt her face, Mossycoat closed Polly's right eye lid and into her left eye poured the remainder of the powder, which began to eat its way into her eye as if the grains were not petal dust and grit but motivated little teeth fizzing like salt through the lipid layer of her eyeball then down, down—

Polly screamed—

The next she knew, she was walking beside Tom on the lane up from Cinderhill and her house was in view.

Afterwards, Polly could not believe how fast the world splintered on her and Tom.

Whatever bluntness of memory and emotion had settled on them after drinking the tea could not explain such detailed hallucinations. Their time in the woods and under the earth could not be true. The rational world laid on its calming hands. The chance what they'd experienced was real found its comfortable seat in explanation in reason; in the ironically safe little catch-all term of *drugs*. That night was a trick of the light, and for Polly – still 'stoned' – the sight of a blue flashing light outside her parents' house was all it took to stow the experience under a chair.

Yet it was not hidden; the world was no longer safe—

This was apparent as soon as she opened the back door to find everyone awake at eleven in the evening. The PC in the car had followed them in wordlessly, and the WPC who was sat reading by the telephone put her book down and stared.

"I've hurt my eye," Polly said. "I can't see anything from my eye."

Her mother stared, unmoving. She looked furious. In contrast, her father was on her in a second, holding her, and in another moment he'd pulled Tom in as well.

"Your eye?" her mother said. "Your fucking eye?

Her father pulled her in tighter. "You've been gone three days, Polly" he whispered. He was bony. She could feel his ribs. How had he lost so much weight? "Jesus," he said. "Where have you been?"

"We were in the woods. Dad, I can't see out of my eye."

Tom said, "Three days? We were at the house this lunchtime."

"What house?" asked her mother—

When Polly was younger, about ten, she'd crept downstairs late at night because from below she'd heard strange voices, sounds. Through the jamb of the door, she saw her mother talking to a woman called Jane who owned the stables in Cinderhill. Polly had never heard another human so broken, her voice like a hay bale in a hurricane, unable to hold any form or structure. Gradually, the woman managed to get out that she'd been driving north on the bypass when her horsebox had come apart on the road. The horse had hit the tarmac standing at about fifty miles per hour, his legs shattering. "Like twisting a fistful of dry spaghetti in your hands," Jane said. "And his noises. Pieces of him on the road. For fifty yards. His bones still trying to run away."

Polly had crept back upstairs, the horror of what she'd heard somehow held apart from her howling into her pillow. She knew nothing of the theory of vicarious trauma then – wouldn't for some years – but for months afterwards, and at less regular intervals for years, she saw the horsebox disintegrate and the horse stagger as the axle gave, the horsebox wall twenty yards behind the bed already, and then step from the sloping floor of the horsebox bed onto the tarmac speeding beneath—

And again, again. The accident was not something she'd ever seen, but she saw it over and over.

A similar thing now happened to her life. It came apart astonishingly fast. Fifteen years of sheltered safety gave way to speed and danger that shattered everything—

In the three days they'd been gone, Alan Stuckey had had a complete nervous breakdown. To have lost his wife had holed him beneath the waterline already, but the idea his son was similarly gone sunk him entirely, and he'd been committed to the Mind asylum.

"He's not getting out," her father said.

Tom confirmed this when he came to see her the next day. "They say I'm going into a home. Like an orphanage or something. I can't go into a home. I just can't."

Below, Polly could hear her mother shift into a higher gear of invective, her father's evenness of tone just about audible underneath.

"I think she blames me," Tom explained. He looked at her shadowy form on the bed in the darkened room. "Is this my fault?"

To help her damaged eye, the lights were off and the curtains drawn, which considering the blistering weather was perverse: her bedroom was a heated gloom. Polly didn't dare shake her head, but she couldn't speak.

"How's your eye?" Tom asked gently.

She'd been told not to cry but the simple fact of him asking caused her eyes to fill then spill from the sides of the bandages. "The doctor said I might be blind in that eye. Forever. It doesn't respond to the light."

Tom slipped his hand into hers.

Her parents wouldn't take him in. Her father told her this. She could sense her mother standing behind him, whether literally or figuratively she could not tell under the bandages. She begged them. *Don't make him go into a home.*

"We've no room," he father said. "Where would he sleep?"

The next day Tom came she asked him about the time they spent under the hill.

"I guess we were drunk," he said.

"We can't have been drunk in the same way," she replied. "Do you remember the coffin?"

"Yes."

"And the sunny day deep underground? All the cats?"

"Yes. Cats were everywhere."

"And the boy. That tall gold boy?"

"I remember," Tom replied.

"Do you remember the woman with the sharp teeth?"

"I do," he said, quietly. "I remember."

"Why didn't she get you?"

He was silent for a moment. "I don't know. I was higher than you on the stair. She got to you first. I was pulled into a room of women and they hid me." His speech was full of pauses, creaks and hesitancies. "One was so beautiful. Tall and blonde. She lay on top of me then—. All the other women lay on top of her. They were heavy—. Not individually. But together." Polly heard him shuffle on his seat. "I heard muttering. Then the woman on top of me said, *Tell her he's been claimed. Tell her I've named him*—. *Tell her this*. Her mouth was next to my ear. So loud. I heard the women above us repeat the message—. More and more muffled. And—."

He fell silent. Polly said, "Go on."

"I don't know how it happened but my clothes were off. I don't know how it happened. I think they took them off. My thing—. And her area—. They were close together then—." He sighed, deeply. "She wiggled about something chronic."

"Are you kidding?" she yelled. "Are you kidding me?"

Polly screamed at him. The anger was an unclogging of her confusion and helplessness at the utter perversion of their lives in a matter of hours. Her anger was both unfair and fair, doubtless therapeutic, yet even in the moment she understood to have let him bear the flood was selfish. She screamed, barely even words until she realised she could no longer hear him, and she could no longer hear him because he had left. He never came back.

She found out he'd gone missing the following day. Social services had come to collect him, but he was not at home. *The horse staggers sideways on the collapsing horsebox chassis and takes a fatal step onto the bypass.*

Days passed with no sign. The police came to ask her where he was. Was there a hiding place they had? They dredged the river, sent search parties through the woods. She learned from the lead police officer, Ian Bucknall, that the Littlegoods had been interviewed – everyone had been interviewed, even school friends they'd not seen for weeks – but no one had any information.

By this time, the newspapers were involved, and the details they had were crooked, wrong, words from another tale. One local paper assured them that Tom's bike had been found in the lane to Cinderhill, scant yards from his house, the front wheel turning idly as if it had just been abandoned. There were burn marks in a nearby field. They were spaced widely as if they were the legs of a landing craft.

"People have lost their minds," her father said.

It was claimed the police had found a black half-smoked Sobranie cigarette – a *Russian* cigarette – with garish red lipstick visible on the golden filter, Tom the child-victim of a Soviet *femme fatale*. Such speculations, in another context, might have been hilarious, but Polly was in no doubt the truth she *knew* was even more ridiculous.

A week passed. Polly's guilt grew damaging to her mind, and her ability to remain unbroken was challenged. She'd been careful when talking to the police. She'd told them about the abandoned cottages by the bypass, which she knew they'd searched.

"And you know about the Littlegood place," she said.

As time went by, doubt settled in as to whether or not Tom had in fact run away. It was the police's first theory because they knew he did not want to go into a home, but Tom had nowhere to go, and more and more Polly felt certain the only place he would have gone was the Littlegood house, which is where doubt took root, because Ian Bucknall from the police, as well as her parents, had sniffed around the house in the woods as if Peter and Elfy were Childsnatchers Royale.

Questions turned on how no one could explain a three-day absence. *Drugs*, her mother thought. *Abuse*, the police did not *quite* say. Polly had not mentioned the tea, the wild night, the truth behind her wounded eye. At first it was the difficulty of finding the words because every last English one of them would find her mother's scorn. All she had was an adolescent's insistence on half-truth—

We went to the Littlegood house and got lost on the way back. We were only gone twelve hours.

Yet as the days passed, the frank disbelief the adults had for her was a fertile soil for Polly's doubt. *Perhaps we were kept captive*, she thought. Perhaps all she knew to be the truth of that night was confection, her mind papering over an horrific memory with another reality. But then how could there be any correlation between what she and Tom had experienced? They'd talked. They shared the same memories. They could not have shared the same dream.

The police searched the Littlegood place again. "This time for a body," her mother said. Nothing was found.

One night, Ian Bucknall was at the house late. He lived in the settlements and often dropped in on his way home. Polly had that day seen some improvement in the vision of her left eye: indistinct shapes moving that she knew from the evidence of her good eye was her dad cooking.

Whether it was relief, weariness or dread for Tom, she finally told all. The tea, the graves, Robin, the sense of human creatures in the circle of trees, the explosion of their minds and the vertical village hidden under a tree trunk in Murdered Wood—

"The graves are false," she said. "Did you check the graves? If you searched and didn't find him, maybe he was in one of the graves?"

Her mother's face was stone.

"We've gone over the ground with radar," Ian said. "The graves were opened days ago, the second time we searched the house—." He told them the police had held Peter for three days. With menace he added, "He'd have told us anything he knew." The police had threatened to charge him with kidnap, murder. They'd even threatened to make Elfy his accomplice, but Peter had insisted his innocence.

"He said you'd been around, helping them, being neighbours. He said Tom was helping clear out a shed?"

"Yes."

"And you helped out as well. He said something about soap."

"Yes."

"He told us he'd never served you or Tom anything narcotic. We checked the house." He paused. "There's *no* evidence of any wrongdoing, and *all* the evidence we need that Tom ran away and we don't know where he is."

"It was Robin who made the tea," she said. "I never said Peter made the tea. Robin made the tea. It was Robin who cut Tom's arm." She was crying now, hard and outstared by Ian and her parents. "It was him," she said. "I know it."

"Robin's backward," said Ian. "He's a fucknut."

Polly stared at the police officer. She didn't know how to reply. To deny his statement was not within reach, and now everything was revealed, she saw how completely she'd failed her parents and Ian Bucknall from the police. It wasn't simply that they thought she was damaged. They thought she was lying.

"Is there anything you have to tell us?" Ian asked.

His voice was quiet. Her mother stood, furious. Polly knew a whole conversation she'd not been privy to was in the room with them. Ian, without looking, clicked his fingers and pointed at Jo to sit down, which she did. Her compliance frightened Polly more than anything.

"Now's the time to tell us, Polly," he continued. "Is there anything you need to say about where Tom might be?"

They think I've done something to him, Polly thought.

"No."

They held each other's eyes for a long moment. Ian nodded. "I didn't think so."

He stood to leave. Jo followed him out—

"She's five foot nothing, you bloody fool," she hissed. "What's wrong with you? What the hell did you think she could have done to a strapping lad like Tom?"

Polly looked up at her dad. "What will happen now?"

"I think they'll stop looking," replied her dad after a moment. "I think the case is closed."

"They can't stop looking."

"He's a runaway."

"He's not a runaway," she said, voice broken.

Her father nodded and did not reply.

The next morning, a woman called Shirley was at the house. She looked like a badger in drag. "I'm here to talk about the troubles you've been having," she sang. "Your fantasies."

Polly didn't know if her first impression was the strain of the previous weeks or a realistic appraisal, but the counsellor was the last strange straw. The woman looked less real than her memories of the great night under the ground. Entitled, supercilious as a cat and permanently aggrieved, Shirley was a horror too far—

Polly didn't say another word about the night. Shirley lasted three sessions before Tony ordered her gone.

"She's a misery hound," he said, "and I'm not feeding my daughter to her. I will not have her made mad."

In silent thanks, Polly put on false cheer and told them she'd decided to look forward. "There's work to do," she said. "It's 'O' Level year. I want to put the past behind me."

In a short time, her parents accepted her feelings, even welcomed them. Tom was closed, the case closed. He was a runaway. There were thousands each year, maybe tens of thousands. Although she knew in her bones and water that, though he would have certainly run, he would never have remained hidden, she managed to make an unsteady peace with his disappearance. In her mind, a small scar-door formed over the memory. The great and wild night had the quality of a dream now, a dream given only one wobble—

It was months afterwards, closing in on Christmas. Her mother handed her a tiny wicker basket. When Polly opened it, she found on a pad of moss at the base the gold jug from the old kettle at the abandoned house. The jug she'd let Tom have. To the handle of the basket was tied a scrap of dirty paper with one word written on it in a bad hand—

polllee

"Where did you get it?"

"It was left on the doorstep." Her mother smiled. "I think you have an admirer."

Polly was cold, cold. "I don't." She swallowed. "Did you see him? What did he look like?"

"Not well. Grey. Had a cold maybe. His dad was dapper, though. Dressed for a black-and-white ball. Very smart. Black suit from head to toe but his pocket lining was red. Probably on their way to a party."

Polly was white, white. "They left me this gold jug?"

"Yes." Jo paused. "Are you okay?"

Cold, white, Polly forced a grin. "I'm fine," she said.

"And it's not gold," her mother added. "It's brass. It's not worth anything. Cute though."

Out in the dark, dark night, beyond the gate that led onto Pook Farm land, the cows lowed and started to run into the greater blackness at the foot of the field.

II

In her early thirties, Polly was idling around a charity shop in Leominster when a title on the bookshelves caught her eye. The book was called *Where the Wasteland Ends* by Theodore Roszak. The title looked hot to her, immediately bringing to mind the engraving on one of the false tombstones at the Littlegood house.

The book had no connection she could see to the grave. It was an exploration of the romantic sensibility, rooted in the sixties and seventies ways of viewing the world. She enjoyed the book, picked up *The Making of a Counterculture*, finding that – like Joan Didion or George Orwell – Roszak had the peculiar knack of finding the *always-true* that made his ideas revelatory far beyond the time he was writing. It gave her an unsettling sense the world turned not in Mayan circles of time but in generational time. The same cycles played out again and again; human existence was simply a matter of switching out the nouns in a repeated text, like replacing light bulbs for newer ones in the same damp old house.

The find led her down a literary rabbit hole for a good few months – Kathleen Raine's *Defending Ancient Springs*, Neil M. Gunn's *The Well at the World's End* – but the title on the spine-creased old Faber paperbound book would not move on. *Where the Wasteland Ends.* The sight of the words tore open the scar-door that had formed over her memory, and from out of the hole seeped blood.

For years, the night she and Tom were lost rarely came to mind. Other events took their place, and as time went on she began to think of that time as the hallucination her parents had decided it must be. At university she'd even called on the experience as evidence of her sophistication around drugs, embedding that night in a magic mushroom narrative. Yet she could not dwell on it. To look at what happened overlong was to come hard up against the oddest fact: the difference in their perception of time. She had not been away for three days yet all external evidence was that she had been. No resolution or explanation was possible.

Her parents had been altered permanently by those three days of absence – her father became nervous where he never had been before; her mother never lost her air of suspicion and affront at not being told the secret – and this change settled in Polly's stomach like a glowing bulb of guilt. At some point she accepted she'd never know where they'd been. The best guess was that they'd been asleep at the Littlegood house while the effects of whatever Robin had given them wore off, each of them exploding with dreams.

Tom was another matter though. Thoughts of Tom could take her off at the knee. A man the same height as him standing near her plugged her right back, a plug with a seventeen-year lead slotting into a seventeen-year-distant socket. Tom came to her in dreams. He came to her on station platforms when trains pulled out, and she experienced the sight of a passenger behind the moving glass as Tom's face in the coffin as it twisted upwards. She waited for trains facing away now.

The narrative everyone believed – that he'd run away rather than be put in a home, a statistic – could not be true. Yet he had never resurfaced, and somehow she could not see him on the streets of Bristol or London. She didn't believe he would have run in that way. There was not enough time to have passed for him to reach that level of desperation. Unless, and she hated to think of it, he was dead.

The Roszak book brought a detail to mind, a detail that had vanished on her in the closing of the door. Tom's dream of being in a grave – *A Hare* – with someone tugging at his shirt from below, and his dream of *Where the Wasteland Ends* standing open, stairs leading down. She knew Tom had gone to the Littlegood house. She knew this was why she'd finally told the police to go there, thus pulling the thread in her own life and putting a ladder in her sanity that ever remained visible. Yet they'd searched the house in the woods and found nothing in the house or the false graves. Nothing had been found.

"It's like I've forgotten something," she told her counsellor, "and so the words *Where the Wasteland Ends* catch me every time I see them on the bookshelf."

"Chuck the book," he replied.

"No. That's——. I like the book."

"Turn the spine to the wall."

"And ruin the line and look of my shelves? It's like we haven't met, Graham." She paused. "It's the sense I've left something undone. Like I forgot to lock a door, or meet someone, or pick something up. A mental itch. It's the not knowing."

"Tom."

"Yes."

"Guilt?"

Polly took a long while with this—

"I don't know. I think I got off better than him. Without knowing, it's hard to judge. But if I'd spoken out earlier, they might have found him. In the graves. If that's where he was. And whatever happened to him wouldn't have happened."

"Something else would have happened," said Graham.

"What?"

"Life."

"I'm not sure if you're trying to make a profound point or that's the most facile statement that came to mind."

The counsellor smiled. "I'm not going to pick that up, Polly."

"I do feel guilt," she said quietly after a moment. "All the time." She paused. "He asked if it was all his fault. It wasn't. And I didn't answer him. I should have answered him. So there is guilt. Whatever it was that happened. I feel guilt—

"Before, it was buried. Not well. It came to mind in dreams. And sometimes I had to put it aside with effort. But now I think of that time every day. I *over*think of that time until it feels obsessive. Needless, but necessary. I can't put it out of mind in the way I once did. It's become too heavy. And all because I saw that book – a book with sod all relevance – in a charity shop.

"I need to know what I did wrong. I keep going over the steps. I should have spoken out. Earlier. I've should have gone out there to the Littlegood house—."

"My *should* alarm is flashing into overdrive."

"Your *should* alarm is too sensitive. Sometimes people just need to speak, Graham."

"Okay." The counsellor paused. "You couldn't have gone out there. That was when you hurt your eye, wasn't it?"

"Yes." Polly was silent a long while. "I know these aren't rational thoughts, but they are my thoughts. I don't know what's happened these last few months but it's driving me crazy. I think of Cinderella. In one telling of the tale her step-mother mixes three bowls of lentils together. I think I had the past sorted like those three separate bowls of lentils, but for some reason they're mixed and I have to sort them back out. I have to sort out those bowls back into brown, green, yellow. What's true, what's false. What I did wrong."

"The truest version of events is not necessarily the one that puts you in the worst light."

Polly sat with that statement for minutes, and the counsellor let her. "Thank you," she said at last. "That's a sentence I'll keep." She paused. "The word *necessarily* is the most important word there, isn't it?"

The counsellor made a sound he often made with Polly, a tiny exasperated moan that sounded as though he was trying to say *No* and *Yes* and moo all at the same time. She laughed at him.

Polly liked Graham. She'd been seeing him off and on for a year, her original pull to counselling being a sense after a visit to a friend with children that there was a person missing, a non-existent child. It was the oddest feeling, not ovarian nudge so much as a subconscious sense she'd left *someone* behind. Although focused on her career in charity administration, and suspicious her friends' glee at her perceived broodiness was their sublimated drive to lure her toward the same trap they'd fallen into, Polly could not put aside the moments when her body – not her mind – felt a momentary panic she'd forgotten a person who was not there.

Connecting this to Tom had taken a laughably short amount of time in her sessions with Graham. It had been their second session when he'd asked who she *had* left behind in her life, and the great night had come out of her like pop from a shook bottle. Yet once told, the tale slid to the background, and as Graham tried neither to guide nor advise, so Tom returned to being a figure standing in the shadows of her life. Now he was again lit—

Graham was right about the eye. The eye was the part of the story that would not fit. The narrative that everyone wanted to believe, in varying shades of sinister, was that Tom and Polly had imbibed something, slept three days at the Littlegood house, driving Tom's father insane, which led to Tom's running away—. This tale was undermined by the eye detail. It was her first experience of knowing something to be true but the world not accepting it. There was no explanation. It had not been the result of a knock or a jab or a chemical. Medicine was stumped.

There had been great improvements in function. Her experience was of a certain muddiness of vision in that eye, not wholly corrected by a visibly thicker lens in her glasses or the prescription for drops to pin the pupil. Reading for any length of time caused her to have blind spots, some large – areas of travelling pink that might block out significant portions of text – and if she drank, the damaged eye drifted perceptibly out of true. There had even been lengths of time when she'd been blind again in that eye, and although she'd become used to the affliction, she'd never had a satisfactory explanation. The finest she'd heard was a consultant in London who pulled a rueful face and said, "Where your eye is concerned, sometimes we just have to accept that's just how that bird sings, you know?"

Neither was it entirely true that her dislocation with the present was new. It had come and gone. There had been moments in nature when from one step to the next the trees and flowers had seemed to take special notice of her as she passed by, as if the world had glowed with pleasure at her presence. It never happened abroad, but on the peninsula and elsewhere in Britain, she felt she walked through a doorway invisible to all and the woods became peopled with the unseen.

One vivid experience on Hampstead Heath came to mind. She had walked up from her hall of residence at Westfield College to meet a friend. It was her first year at university, and she'd never walked there alone before. Night fell faster than expected, and her friend was not where she expected him to be. This was in 1989, there were no phones, so she had no choice but to wait in the growing dark at the edge of the trees. The sense came she was watched, eyes behind the trees, and the feeling dragged her straight back to the Littlegood house in its perfect henge of living wood, the dark inside the trees glowering and so familiar to her that she felt both terror and the odd safety that comes from being on home turf.

Then she saw lights in the depths of the trees, flickering like candles being carried, the quivering light blinking on and off as the flames passed behind the trunks. Now and then a tiny glimmer of face stared directly at her with curiosity. The sight felt like a ritual she had no business seeing, a ritual that might bring death to infidel eyes. The vision reminded her of waking at seven or eight years old in the middle of a night journey to Scotland to see a giant Catherine wheel turning in a square in a nowhere urban environment, shrouded figures all around, a split second glimpse into ancient terror her child mind could neither explain nor forget. A glimpse out of this world into another only to find people lived there, and lived according to a moral code she could not hope to understand.

Yet in Hampstead, she found a truth that rattled her to the bones. Only her bad eye saw the lights. She closed her bad eye and the woods returned to dark. The eye blinded by Mossycoat could see the lights in the trees—

As the days following her session with Graham went on, disturbance became unhappiness became a persistent anxious slowness that rattled more days than it left alone. *Where the Wasteland Ends.* One night she dreamt vividly of that extraordinary gold boy with Peter's face and Elfy's ears. He was in an abandoned building, nothing in any of the rooms bar peeling wallpaper and rotten floorboards. Tom and Robin had gone to explore the rooms. A toilet, bowl only, stood in the centre of the big room. Polly was in need and the gold boy was panicked as the other two had not returned. He left the room to let Polly go to the loo, but when she looked, she'd filled the bowl with black piss that would not flush because there was no flush. The black piss filled the bowl so perfectly there was a meniscus on the top, and she began to get frantic. To have her bowl of black piss seen was more shaming than could be endured. Yet none of the boys returned. They were not in the other rooms. Polly was alone.

"What do you think it means?" she asked Graham.

"Christ with the dreams," he replied. "I think it means you needed the loo."

Yet he was there. Tom was there. Robin was there. Three unreal boys: prince, pauper and rat, like archetypes in her dreams.

By chance, a few weeks later her parents were moving to Sevenston to be closer to medical support, and she surprised them by offering help. Neither was frail, but they accepted gladly. Polly rarely came home. She asked to stay on for a few days in the empty house, a guardian until the new owners returned from Hong Kong to take up residence.

"You're looking, aren't you?" asked her dad as he took a last look around the bare house. "This is about Tom."

"Yes."

"Where were you those three days?" he asked. "You always said you didn't know."

She got close to him. "Everything was as I said, dad. We never slept and it was an afternoon and an evening. I don't know what to tell you." She put her arms around him. "Nothing happened. The world went odd and then everything went to shit. There's no explanation."

"You tell me if you could?"

"I'd tell you in a heartbeat if I knew anything other than what I know. I always told you both the truth, even when you didn't want to listen." She paused. "Did you ask Mr Gloyn if I could call him?"

"Yes. He's waiting. Remember how old he is."

Through Mr Gloyn she managed to trace Elfy. She could not face going back to the Littlegood place, and she'd already discovered Peter still lived there. Mr Gloyn traced her to an isolated cottage a mile from Hollow Thomas. He laughed when she called her Elfy. "Her real name is Gail Snook," he told her. "I mean, yikes. No wonder she changed it."

Her cottage was beautiful, old stone and thatch. The ground descended from the front door in lines to a stream, across which ran a wooden bridge with clutches of daffodils either side of the steps up. To hear the stream mutter all night long must be one of those deep country treasures, Polly thought, the hidden language of water that a sleeping human mind would gradually come to understand a little of as the years went by.

The garden held vegetables. Flowers clung to the odd functionless spaces, ornament only where nothing useful might grow. Toward the edge of the small property stood a pottery shed at river level. Rejected pots stood in disgrace on shelves outside, and the base of the hut showed Elfy's studio had flooded regularly. As a possible future for herself, Polly thought it near perfect.

Now she was here, she found it hard to go in and say hello. In the years between, it was her shaming of Elfy that had caused her the most pain. Her intoxication couldn't excuse it. It was one of those moments in her life that could always send her into squirming horrors of embarrassment if it came to mind. *Your dagnabbits.* The way she'd covered her chest up might be seen in a woman at work, or a similar look of confused hurt might come over the face of a boyfriend in a quarrel and hot hot shame would physically make Polly writhe. Perversely, of all the parts of that dreadful day, it was her closing of Elfy that caused her agonies, and to be in a place where she might usefully apologise scared her.

The paralysed moment was broken by the woman herself. She'd seen her visitor and come from the cottage.

"Hello?"

Polly's presence was a shock. Elfy covered it well, but Polly was alive to emotional nuance and could tell the woman had stiffened in a way that never let up for the remainder of her visit.

"You're a woman," Elfy said when some tea was made and lavender, walnut and apricot cake served. "How old are you now?" She shook her head. "Don't answer that. How old am *I*? That's the question in my head."

Elfy was identical, no weight gained and few lines. A lot of confidence had sapped, but she had seen the same faltering of nerve in her parents as they'd aged. The only difference was a line of grey hairs across her forehead, and Polly wondered if those hairs took the strain when the woman's hair was pulled into a ponytail, as if human hair could be tuned to a grey note.

They talked of the cottage, the river, the seasons, the time passing, Polly's work in charity administration, Elfy's ceramics and open studio events. A wary rhythm settled in, few awkward silences or those moments of grim-grin hungering for a conversational opening, like threading a needle when the end of the cotton has split. The truth was they didn't really know each other. Polly had spent the bulk of her time that distant summer with Peter. A generous tallying of the time she and Elfy had spent in meaningful interaction could be measured in minutes. Yet between them, as the conversation deepened, what they talked about turned tighter and tighter around the connecting point.

"I keep looking at your eye," Elfy said at one point. "The police kept asking about——. Sorry. Your pupils are two different sizes."

"I've drops I need to take otherwise the pupil shrinks to nothing."

"Can you see out of it?"

"I don't notice it. I can't read for long lengths of time. People say that eye drifts if I've been drinking." She paused. "I sometimes see odd things."

"It's a pity about not being able to read for long," Elfy said. "Peter thought you were destined to be an academic. *A little Lorna Sage*, he called you."

Polly nodded slowly. "What happened with Peter?"

"Age difference." Elfy paused. "Lots of things. But at the heart——. My mother always said, *Twenty and thirty-five isn't the same as thirty-five and fifty*. I think we stayed together a good couple of years needlessly because I didn't want my mother to be right. Do you get paid for charity administration?"

The conversation progressed in this hesitant fashion. Polly recalled the kettle she and Tom had unearthed. The talk was a similar decanting. Nearly everything they spoke of was conversational soil and shard – healthy, life giving but little there of lasting worth – yet now and again a detail or word would be placed before them that glowed with emotional value. Each of them understood and recognised that glow. *The perfect bottle. The shining animal skull. The golden jug.* They tumbled from the conversation, sometimes accidentally, sometimes placed, and the two women took hold of them – or not – as they were unearthed. The first mention of Peter was one such. *The house* was another. More oblique conversational artefacts like *back then* and *that summer* and once, so perfect and snatchable, *the boys.* When Elfy said *the boys* Polly wanted to bite her tongue out, but she waited, waited.

Elfy disclosed she sold her pottery in Peter's shop, which spoke of an amicable parting—

"Someone said he was wealthy."

"Yes. Stupidly so." Elfy waved a hand to indicate the cottage. "This is all mine. I don't owe anything on it. The separation was a good one. Once we decided to part, we had one of those talks. *An Occam's razor talk*, Peter said. The paperwork took months but communicating openly what we wanted on leaving took two hours and three bottles of red."

"And Robin?"

The name had not been directly spoken, but Polly felt it was there on the table between them. Elfy looked at her directly then declined the opening—

"Peter started selling his stuff more widely. I think a woman with a bit of clout was using his salve for something. In the space of a couple of years the whole thing blew up. High-end London outlets, famous women loved it. People travelled to his shop in Huntsham-in-the-moor, which is not exactly central." From the old Dutch dresser she pulled out a tin. "I did the logo."

Polly picked up the tin. She was greatly surprised to find she knew it. She'd even treated herself to a hand cream a few years ago. It had been an expense so great it had caused her a psychic wound for days afterwards. Across the lid was the *sans serif* logo.

"Peter is *PiG?*"

"Yes." Elfy beamed, the first unhindered smile she'd let leave her face. "It was supposed to be *PLG* but when I did the logo I made the *L* lower case. People misread it and the name stuck."

"I'm gobsmacked."

"The company is *PLG* but everyone calls it *PiG*. The money rolls in. The products never seem to go out of style." She faltered. Something about that open tap of money made her uncertain, then she rallied. "You should visit," she said brightly. "He'd love to see you."

The danger of this statement held the silence for a long moment—

"I called the police on him," Polly said. "On both of you."

"Yes."

"I can imagine anger."

Elfy nodded. "Some." After a moment she added, "It terrified him. They terrified him." A glint of bitterness searched out toward Polly. "They hurt him. Physically. Not like you hear about from abroad. *It was British violence*, he said. But he had bruises on him. On his face." Polly wasn't about to apologise. "Where were you?" Elfy asked. "Where did you go for three days?"

"We were under the ground," Polly said. "And it wasn't three days. My memory is we tried to walk out of the wood. You pointed out the houses to us. But then there were people in the trees. They took us both under the ground." Polly was looking at Elfy levelly now. "I've told myself for years we were stoned on mushrooms or something, but it's not true, is it? It can't be true because it wasn't just me who experienced the night underground. It was also Tom. I know because we talked before he vanished." She leaned forward. "I know he came to you when he realised he'd be going into a home. What happened with Tom?"

There it was. From the mass of word-soil that comprised a human conversation – *this* human conversation – the little golden jug had at last tumbled out.

"There are so many parts," Elfy said, soft. "And also nothing to say. I don't know where to start." She looked up then, eyes naked. "Stay. I'll open a bottle."

"It's four o'clock."

Elfy didn't reply. She simply stared at Polly.

"Tom came to the house afterwards," Polly said.

"Tom came to the house afterwards," Elfy agreed.

She went to get wine. Polly tried to get comfortable. The act was futile. She was itching to smoke. Elfy had not blinked when she'd said there were people in the trees and they'd spent a night underground. Whenever she'd disclosed these details, long before she learned never to mention them to anyone, everyone else behaved as though she'd soiled herself in public. Whatever the truth was, Elfy believed. *Elfy believed her.* It was this realisation that made Polly begin to shake. She took her cigarettes from her bag and lit one without asking permission.

Elfy started with the graves. Peter home from university with friends, high on Hesse and psychedelics, obsessed with altered states. It was the sixties. He'd stolen or come up with a concept called *the green mind* that held there was a world mind – a nature mind – that surrounded everything, out of which humans had fallen at the birth of consciousness. He believed – millions believed – psychedelic experience plugged the human back into this natural network.

"But he decided there were other ways to re-access this green mind, one of which he thought of as a natural sensory deprivation tank. They'd open up the false graves his grandad had dug. You know what I mean. It was all *The Golden Bough* and the counterculture and stuff." Elfy drank. "Gubbins," she said. "That gubbins. *Gubbins* is a good word.

"Underneath the grass on the graves, there is a thick layer of soil over tarred planks. Lift up the planks and the vault of the grave is below." She drank, refilled her glass. "Peter and his friends went into the graves one by one. Essentially, they'd be buried alive for twelve hours, going in at six in the evening to come out in the morning at six a.m. I did it myself. Much, much later. This was the sixties, seventies. I hadn't met him then, obviously. I'd have been ten, for heaven's sake—

"They spoke of hallucinations, panic attacks, shitting themselves, visions, praying to gods they didn't believe in to rescue them from being buried alive. Even the trust they had in each other to dig them up in the morning crumbled after—. Well, Peter said three minutes. When I did it, it took me to the root of human trust, risk aversion, embedded human truths. I screamed for God, parents and the only response was more silence—

"Peter had life-changing visions down there. He said his friends changed overnight. One went full religious, became a monk. Peter's girl-friend dumped him saying she wanted children and she wanted them now, and she knew he wasn't in that place. One man went very peculiar. He visited once when we were together." She shook her head. "He was like a burnt light bulb. Some deep central essential filament had blown. Something was gone from him.

"But for Peter, he was convinced he'd found access to a world or dimension underground where an entire other race lived. Mad, obviously."

She fell silent. Polly said, "But not mad."

Elfy drank. "No."

To fill the silence, Polly told her what Mrs Tarr said when she was a child. "That curiosity, that belief was in his family. He inherited it."

"Yes. The grandfather did a number on him. Whatever his experience, as far as Peter was concerned, he'd been taken underground to see the little folk."

"You said you went into the grave yourself?"

Elfy nodded. "It was just me and him. By the time I came on the scene, he'd dialled that part of his experience back a lot. We went out there at dusk. Candles. He put the planks back then shovelled the earth over the planks so I was completely buried in a quiet grave." There was a long silence. "That night underground occupies a central part of my life, Polly. It's like my life was growing from my shoulder and then found movement at the elbow, and the elbow joint was that night in the grave. I had absolute trust in Peter, but in the grave the out-of-control eventualities came to mind. *What if he has a heart attack or an aneurysm? What if he's arrested for a crime he didn't commit?* Don't laugh. And that's not the worst of it. My head had tigers coming from out of the grass, a giant eagle carrying Peter off with talons embedded in his shoulder bones. *What if that happened?* Wild, wild reasons why he might be unable to dig me up in the morning—

"And cold. I had blankets down there but the earth is cold even at the height of summer, and there's nothing—. Mud nothing all around you. Peter was right. It's the void. It's the *nothingness that is.*"

Elfy told how panic had settled in. For hours she kept it down, slowly breathing. Each second was ripped from panic solely by mastery of her breath. The breath was the only thing that kept her mind whole, and if any part of her attention slid from her breathing, it came up against the dark mud all around. Her mind was lost to terror. Yet there were also moments of sleep. It was night, after all, and she was tired. The times when she fell a little asleep only to jerk back into wakefulness in a grave felt as dangerous as slipping at the edge of a cliff. Terror. And then one jerk into wakefulness she lost her grip entire. She forgot her breathing. There was screaming, howling, begging, and a smell crawling from her—

"I swear, it was the oddest thing. Like cat musk. What is that? Civet. But sourer, like the stink of fear itself that should never come out of a human, and that smell abandoned my body like a rat from a sinking ship. Some oil that should never see the light of day. Like spinal fluid. That smell came out of me in the grave.

"And I can't explain what happened next. I entered a place between sleeping and waking. Now I think my brain did me a kindness and simply blinked off cold. I heard voices, but not in a mad way. Murmurings of voices I knew. My mum. My dad when I was a kid. The extraordinary safety he put out. I don't know how to describe it. It was like I was hearing him speak in another room.

"And I remembered other times in my life. I recalled a time when my boyfriend-at-the-time's band was on stage. I was maybe nineteen. Shortly before I met Peter. They were called The Toilet Gravies. I mean, the name—. But I always wanted to sing with them.

"One night they were playing and the boyfriend called me up on stage." She drank. "In all honesty, I'd been appalling to him. You know how you are at that age? Just entitled female nastiness. And I thought calling me up to sing was his way of getting me back on side, but it wasn't. It was revenge. I stood at the mic in front of the audience, looking so young and eager, probably—." She shook the image out of her head. "And he said, *Get us four beers, yeah?* And I walked off. And I got those beers." She snorted. "In the grave, that whole memory played in my head over and over, except the scene was ruined because my father was talking behind the wall and in my memory playback the dickhead was getting frustrated because the pain he wanted to cause wasn't connecting. *What's my father saying behind the wall?* I was saying to him. Something in my head was disturbing the playback of a memory I was playing in my head. How twisted and strange is that?

"In and out I went. Vivid dreams, except they weren't dreams. Doors where no doors should be——. I exited that weird hallucination through a round wooden door in the bass drum of the band." Elfy shook her head violently. "Anyway, you don't want to hear this. Nothing more tedious than hearing about another person's trip.

"Time stopped. I screamed myself mute. And gradually the terror ceased. My mood and emotions had found this strange, even swell, like a cradle rocking or waves mid-sea. I don't remember the rest of the time passing. I was changed. In the grave, I was changed for the better.

"And Peter had made me this sort of liquidised drink with spinach, avocado and mint. My God. I sat up in the grave and drank this glass of green straight down. It was like I tasted it with every inch of my skin. I could taste that drink with my feet."

Silence.

"There was a suicide," Elfy said.

"That's terrible."

"It shocked Peter. He stopped the burials cold. He was already into plant-based diets, that sort of thing. The idea of finding the green mind through natural substances took him over. One day, he vanished for three days." Elfy stopped. "That's never occurred to me before. Three days——. Anyway, he returned with a recipe for tea made out of marjoram and other stuff. Some of the ingredients I'd never heard of. It transported him, this tea. I drank it too, but I never went anywhere. Most didn't. For me it was like a doobie buzz, but he'd just——. Vanish.

"The strangest thing was that the night he returned, there were two tracks pressed into the grass like corn circles. They looked like the wheels of a carriage but a carriage couldn't have passed through the trees." Elfy stopped, opened her hands out. "I'm tired. You talk now."

Polly told her of what she'd experienced. Mossycoat, the woods, the helical village under the earth. The coffin, her eye. To speak of it so completely, in a way she never had even with Tom – never had the time for with Tom – was divesting. Watching Elfy watch her, Polly felt like an egg without its shell, but when she'd finished telling the tale, the woman simply replied, "Yes. That. He'd come back with exactly those tales.

"And then came the party. This was months later. I couldn't join in as I was pregnant. A group of friends came and Peter cooked up a huge batch of wild marjoram tea. It was the first time he'd shared it outside of the two of us, and it had never worked for me." She pointed at Polly. "This is significant.

"Soon I saw a few of them chatting away, wandering into the tall grass following God knows what. Little people only they could see. Many were just stoned – the same as had happened with me. Peter and three others *connected*, however. Two of the men returned sodden with sweat. They'd been dancing for six hours. A woman who called herself Sabbath—." She paused, laughed. "It was that time, you know? Sabbath vanished. Peter didn't see her for months. Not that she was gone for months, but she said she'd lived with an underground blacksmith for weeks then woke up walking on the road to Linnet.

"But that night, Peter had the worst trip. I'd never seen him like that. In the night he'd been chastened. *I should never have taken others*, he said. *I'm a Littlegood and only I was given the gift.* He was white. White for days. I was scared for him. It was like he had flu but where the virus was fear. Terror of death. But not like in the grave. A bad death. *I had to make a bargain*, he said. *An agreement. I had to offer something in exchange as surety I'd never share the knowledge with another.* His access to the green mind was his alone, and he'd taken *strangers* to that place. That was the transgression. He never told me what surety he'd offered."

Elfy was silent. After a long minute Polly asked, "To what extent did you believe him? To you—. It must have sounded fantastical."

"Of course. But I was young, and I was saturated in it. I mean, I basically walked into the Littlegood house and from then on the pictures on the walls, the books on the shelves, the prints and his family were all soused in this other world. And I loved him. I loved it. Think of how old I was. I was a baby. And the possibility of new ways of being is seductive to the young. I was sad——. No, I was *devastated* that first time when my trip wasn't the same as Peter's. When I couldn't connect the same way he had. But I also remember thinking maybe it was all in his head. In the grave I spoke to real people in my past. I recognised them. But that was my experience. For another person in the grave, who didn't recognise who came to them in that time of extremis, who knows what explanation and reasons your mind might supply you with? And of course I was pregnant, and other things were on my mind. Real things." She paused. "Is it getting dark already?"

"Tom," said Polly, quiet.

"Yes." Elfy's eyes filled with tears. "What I can tell you won't help you. That afternoon, Tom came to the house as you imagined. He didn't want to go into a home. He thought his father needed time to get better——. Did he?" Polly shook her head. "Tom asked us to buy him this time. But we knew the police would come, so we put him in the grave. *Where the Wasteland Ends*. The police came. Oh my God, they went through the place. The grass, the woods. The bedrooms, the cellar, the sheds. Not the graves, not then, because they didn't know they were false. We were terrified as they were here for hours. Scary shit. But we kept to the story. *You visited, you left*. And when the police were gone, we rolled back the sod and pulled up the planks and Tom wasn't there."

"Could have got out himself?"

Elfy shook her head. "It looks a thin layer, but it's not. The weight of the soil would have been too heavy. And why would he have put it back in place?"

"Where did he go?"

"You know where he went, Polly." Elfy regarded her over the rim of her wine glass. "Peter always told me that about forty thousand years ago people put food, clothing, tools and toolkits in graves to use in the place where the dead were going. It was always assumed it was heaven. *What if this was not true?* Peter would ask. *What if the place they were going was further underground?*" She downed the contents of her glass, refilled it.

"I'm so sorry. I wish I had something else to tell you." She paused. "But this is where we are now."

"You believe me," Polly said. "I thought I'd feel happier about finally having someone who believed me."

"And everyone else would think us demented."

"My parents thought it. They hired a shrink. I stopped thinking in terms of my experience. I couldn't trust it. What I knew to be real came hard up against a monolithic belief in the truth of the world. I knuckled under."

"As did I."

"Yes, but I was fifteen," said Polly, sharper than intended.

"Whoopdeedoo," replied Elfy, sharper still. "You were a child and I was a child and Peter was a child and Tom was a child. We're all just children. Adulthood is the greatest faery tale that's ever been told. The fact we're all of us old children is the only human truth!"

Polly kept silent for a time to let the heat disperse. What Elfy had said brought her little. It was a version of a truth she'd always suspected. There was no anger in her now, and part of her understood the woman – the couple – had done the only thing they could. The truth would have sent them to an asylum or gaol.

For Polly this was an intellectual understanding rather than an emotional one, yet there had clearly been a toll. Elfy was alone, and her cottage spoke of loneliness not contentment. The woman was deep into a second bottle, and Polly had only had one glass. Elfy seemed only marginally impaired. She lived at a remove from society. Polly felt for her. The unknowing of how she'd be with Elfy – she foresaw anger, pity – had collapsed to a point of mutual confusion and partial acceptance, but above all care. Polly cared for the woman, which placed one of Polly's truths in a precarious state as she did not know how Elfy would take it if she spoke. To speak might fizzle to nothing, or it might be unspeakably cruel, yet to leave without knowing was impossible, so Polly swallowed and said—

"When we were underground, we met a boy. He looked exactly like Peter and he had your ears."

The loosening came. Elfy wept, an elemental surrender of human restraint, without even the strength to lift her hands from her lap to wipe her eyes. Polly watched her, strangely numb and separate from the downpour. She felt no urge to comfort her, hold her, and this was both a kindness and an unkindness. Polly let her weep.

In time Elfy got out the birth, bringing her child home, a curious lack of connection to the new-born who was perfect and quiet and wonderful and who one morning began to grizzle and sour. There was a diagnosis of post-natal depression, pills that sent her into a little white blurred world until Peter threw them away—

"A part of me knew Robin was not my child. Not my first Robin. A *thing* had been put in his place, a thing that never spoke, learnt letters like an animal and was wrong, wrong."

They could never admit this, however, and there were times when Robin looked like them and was loving and playful so they doubted. The first meetings with doctors and schools gave diagnoses of such unevidenced horrors they decided to home school. This was a decision they made even before *Education Otherwise*, Elfy told her. Yet she knew. She knew the child was not theirs. It was a changeling, and when she'd finally owned that word, screaming it at Peter in a fit of despair, he'd said, *And what can we do? What are either of us to do?* He'd done all he could from the demented books his father and grandfather had collected over the years. Listening at keyholes to hear the baby chatter to its own kin (it didn't), or burning its clothes or cut hair in the fire to hear it squeal (it didn't). Wilder methods to get the child to reveal its true nature—

"Can you imagine how stupid it feels to put beer in egg shells while your kid is asleep?" Elfy hissed. "Can you picture that? That sickening hope your head is telling you is nonsense but your heart thirsts to be true?

"But Robin was a mean child. Which you know. And he could go anywhere. He vanished underground for days, even when he was four years old, and I always knew he was safe and would come back because he was with his people. He was not of this world. But he was all we had. He is all we have.

"Do you know what the oddest thing about that summer is? It's that I finally knew for certain Robin was a changeling. And it's because he wasn't punished for making you the tea. He's one of their own. The knowing is his birthright.

"And if you say there's a boy——. A man." She swallowed. "A man who is my true child. What the hell do I do with that? He'd never know me. And I wouldn't know him."

"Where is Robin now?"

Elfy threw an arm towards the window. "Out there. I haven't seen him in years."

She looked so defeated when she said this, yet Polly had to keep pushing. "I need to go back there. Tom is business I need to finish."

Elfy looked at her. She was drunk now, mean with it. "Like me. Like us. Well, you might just have to live with that, Polly. You can't just go there. There's no magic faraway tree. Only Peter knows the recipe, and he won't tell you. He agreed not to. He offered his life.

"They watch me, you know. I never see them. I never had the ability to see them. That's why the tea never worked on me. But I know they're out there sometimes. When the flowers are around. Springtime. When the world is new." She uncorked a third bottle. "You can stay if you want. Or go. There's no police around here, and there's no one on the roads. So——."

Polly had the sense the night would fast get bloody from here. She collected her things. At the door, she paused and said, "I wanted to apologise. I disrespected you that day. I wasn't fully present but——. I said terrible things about your body."

Elfy didn't have a clue what she was talking about.

Polly risked the road, driving at twenty miles per hour as she knew she was over the limit. The risk seemed worth taking.

The next morning she drove out to Huntsham-in-the-moor. *PiG* was a two-storey house on the outskirts of the town. Polly didn't go in. The lower floor looked like an art gallery with the cosmetic products on plinths, the shop white and unadorned, glass everywhere. For some reason Polly was averse to such shops. They made her sweat for some reason. She'd had a boyfriend who was the same in cookware or china shops: frantically still as the least movement might have broken something and brought the disaster of attention on him. Irrationally, she understood. In smellies shops she imagined the least movement from her body would taint the perfume; some part of her presence in the world would blight the shop.

Over the door was the telephone number, however. She made her way back to the nearest telephone box and put in her 20p. She introduced herself—

"Thank you," Peter sighed into the phone. "I'm so glad you called. Elfy told me you'd visited." He left a few seconds of dead air. "I was worried you'd leave without—. Come into the shop."

"I can't. I'm elsewhere."

"Oh, that's so strange," he breathed. "I'd the strangest sense you were somewhere close." He paused again. "Can we meet?"

"I thought, the house."

"Yes." He breathed again. "I'm stuck here until five though." Hesitantly, he added, "Elfy said she'd spoken to you. At length."

"Yes."

When she didn't elaborate, he replied, "Half five then. At the house."

Polly was agitated when she'd hung up the phone. In her memories, Peter had assumed a position he'd not had when they were together. Then he'd been a mind that attracted her, and even though he was older, considerably so, in later years she'd realised there was a tacit sexual attraction there of which a damaged man might have taken advantage. This meant Peter-in-her-memory had a shadowed glow, and a part of her mind questioned if there was something in him she'd missed: a quality deeper than his innocent intellectual delight in her and his later fear and panicked management of how badly that day had soured.

Hearing his voice brought him back in clear, however: a kindly man, a little buffoony, with that paradoxical blend of obliviousness and acuity she always associated with academia. One who might, on another historical track, have been an avuncular friend she'd drop in on whenever she visited her parents was now an indistinct figure from her past.

Having heard his voice, so familiar and eager, less confident now he was older, she didn't know what to think. Her view of him was doubled, and it was her historic view of him that now seemed the clearer.

Nothing she did took her mind from the meeting so after lunch she decided to drive to the house, safe knowing Peter wouldn't be there for some hours. Parking on the lane in, she left her car in the passing place before walking the woods that circled the house.

The trees were burlier, the light lower. Polly recalled how hot that summer had been, and how live their emotions as they crept through the trees. The house was the same, even down to the bicycle propped unsecured against the wall. It was as if no time had passed within the henge of living wood. It was windy, and Polly reflected again how odd wind was when the place was surrounded by trees.

The studio looked to be a drying room for product now. At the end was an old Albion press. Smoke crawled down the wall but there was no one home. The house was all gloom when she looked in through the windows, and there was no sound.

Polly headed out through the long grass. The giant heads of the sunflowers hung low, bleeding seeds, their petals listless. To be hidden in the grass again was such a pain to her heart and gut because the past – her fifteen-year-old self – seemed right there in her, nested just under her lungs. She stood a long time looking at the graves. *Thistles. A Hare. Where the Wasteland Ends. Low Wedding.* She tried to picture what Elfy had said. Out there in the evening by candlelight, getting into the grave and the munching of the soil as it fell on the planks above. The knowledge police would be beating the grass, searching the house, long lines of them walking the woods. Maybe he'd even heard them above him. The thought this had been Tom's experience was not one she could face. He'd been in there for hours. And the central mystery: he'd vanished and never been seen again, and the only truth of his whereabouts was insane. And yet Polly knew it was not insane.

Tom's dream returned to her again. He was in the grave and fingers tugged at the *back* of his shirt. Polly couldn't even think of it without her throat closing—

She took herself off for hours, heading around the property then off to Hundredwood, which she passed twice before she realised the trees she was walking past in increasing bewilderment was there in front of her in the sixteen, seventeen years' worth of new growth. It was here that they'd walked down into the earth, yet all trace of the boles cut close to the ground was gone, and what remained was a wood grown crooked and gnarled to fill the area.

The more Polly stared, the stranger it looked. New Hundredwood's difference from the trees surrounding was stark. It made Polly think of those webs spun by spiders high on cocaine, LSD, caffeine. Some branches grew down, limbs twisted into knots, and trunks veered sideways as if dodging a bullet. Yet it was beautiful, and under the canopy, the path almost impassable, was the coolest calm she had experienced in a long while.

At five she walked back to the old house to find the back door open and an older, greyer, but essentially the same Peter standing there throwing tea leaves into the compost heap. "I got cover," he said. "You've been here a while," he added, indicating towards her car with his head.

"I went for a walk. This place is the same."

She looked him over. *He must be a millionaire*, she thought, but he was still the same absent scruff. The ponytail was gone.

"You're nervous to be back," he said, a statement.

"Yes," she replied, but in the moment of replying – and largely because he had *seen* her nerves – she was no longer nervous.

Polly stepped inside the house.

"I have something," he said. "It was in the cellar. I kept it."

She sat at the kitchen table and pulled apart the tissue paper. It was a stack of soap, riven with fissures but still fragrant. "This isn't the soap we made."

"It is."

"Is it any good?"

With a tone of grudging surprise he said, "It's okay."

The sight of the soap lit an anger in her. It was not rational, but the gift of the soap took her wrongly. She closed the tissue paper.

Over the space of an hour she told Peter about her experiences that evening and in the night. She could see he understood and accepted everything she had to say as the truth. He gave her encouragement—

She then told him everything Elfy had told her. She told him the feeling she had about leaving all unfinished and her need to have an ending. She told him she knew Elfy and Peter would not have done anything to Tom; that there was no dark thought in her head that they'd weighted his body down and sunk it in the river, or eaten him, or any of the thousand cruelties that might have been in her head on wakeful nights at three in the morning—

"I need to have an ending. And you have the key. If key there is, you hold it, Peter."

Peter was silent for a long moment. Outside night had fallen, the long grass and drear sunflowers waving in the wind. A latch ticked out there in the darkness, and a creature, large and thud-footed, passed by the back door.

"I have a key," he said at last. "And I've used it many times to go looking for Tom. I've never found him. The place we both know—." He looked at her significantly. "That place is as big as the world we live in. It's like a tree, whose roots extend as far beneath as they do above. It is fruitless to look, and I have to go alone."

"Why?"

"Elfy told you why."

"Your family has a connection."

Peter frowned. "Oh, Mrs Tarr. Yes, but that's just where we are. It's not the Littlegood family but more—." He paused. "The veil is thin here. A step off the path—. Cross a bridge across the river at a certain level of light—." He caught Polly's face and smiled. "I know you're angry with me. Us. And you've a right to be. But there was not a *right* way that we failed to see or refused to take. Polly, God knows I'm sorry but also—. I'm not sorry at all."

Silence.

"That thought has occurred to me," said Polly. "That there was no right way. But we were children."

Peter grinned. "Elfy said she answered you on that point."

"Yes," replied Polly. "But still—."

"If a bad thing happens to you as a child, the nearest adult standing gets the kick in the slats?"

Polly held her ground. "Yes."

"I'm not sure I agree with that point of view, Polly."

Silence.

In the absence of sound and the low light, the thud-footed creature passed by the back door again and settled under the window. Over the trees, in the striated dusk of late autumn, the full moon shone down.

"I know this area for miles around," said Peter. "From an early age I was out on my own. You and Tom were the same. Leave the house at nine in the morning and no one knew where I was until teatime. And they didn't worry. Any harm that befell me was schooling. *Nature is a school*, my grandfather told me. *It grades you according to luck and quick thinking. It prizes the ability to think yourself back into the sunshine.*" He busied himself with the kettle on the stove. "When I was in my teens, I went out at night. I loved it. The moonlight and the woods. I'd go for miles, be out for hours. My mother would grumble, but my grandfather knew it was necessary. That aloneness is vital to an adolescent." He widened his eyes. "To suffer my terrible adolescent anguish. Even now when I dream, whole nights I spent outside as a child slide in as backdrops to my adult dream. A crooked tree through which the moon is shining. The way the high hedges divide the light so your head can see the moonlit fields turning to fog, frost, and everything is silver, but your body is walking through the shadows the hedge has cast. All is darkness—

"There's a body of tales here about ghosts, devils, folk. But there's a feature no one pays mind to, which is the high hedges. Nowhere else in the country has them, and they distort the sound of your footsteps. And it's been thought this is the root of all these stories where a maid or a farm boy is walking home after dark only to hear footsteps behind that stop shortly after he or she stops. An echo. Your own footsteps are walking there in the dark behind you, a split second behind. No idea if it's true, but those footsteps—. I remember them. In the night, no tractors or animals to disturb the quiet, I would hear my own footsteps behind me." He put a cup of Earl Grey in front of her. "Or the footsteps of another—

"I was a wild kid. It was heavenly. And it was terrifying, and in a moment you might be pitched into an adult world. I remember making aniseed water to dull the noses of the hunt dogs, squirting it in trails to foil the hunt. One day – I was thirteen – the hunt caught me, and in an instant I was surrounded by horses, men with whips screaming down at me, those mighty hunt women. The kind of landed gentry women who have acres of confidence because they know that between their thighs is *England*.

"Or I'd follow a fox for a day. Watching a bird's nest for hours." He shook his head. "One night I was out. I was off to art college and I wanted to have as much time in the country as I could before I left. I was eighteen. The end of summer. I ended up miles away, almost at Hurlston. You know Hurlston?"

"Where the devil threw a stone."

"That's the place. There's a walk along the river there that takes you past Hollow Thomas. It's an ancient way through the avenue of trees. The path holds close to the river the whole way until you get to the wooden bridge by the Owlbridge Yew. You know where I mean?" Polly nodded. "It was dark, and I was tired. And even though I knew where I was, I'd only been there with family and only during the day. The countryside looks different at night—."

He smiled at her, and Polly realised he was himself nervous. There was a great intimacy between them, only low voices and the *tink tink tink* of teaspoons to be heard, along with the thing that breathed beneath the kitchen window.

"So," said Peter. "I'm on the river road, and I meet an old woman dressed in a green suit. She asks me why I'm on the river road so late, so I tell her I'm heading home and she replies, *The river road isn't safe to walk at night*. But I'm eighteen and invulnerable. *I've got to get home*, I say.

"The old woman takes a bundle of something from her pocket. It's a posy, tied with what looks like the soft hair of a child. *I know you*, she says, *you once fixed a tumble nest back safely in a tree. You'll need this against Crowsteer.*"

Peter grinned wickedly when he saw Polly shiver at the tale. He put his head into the steam from his cup. The light was low, and in the lowering of his head he took on the air of a sinister masked creature.

"So," he continued, "I ask who Crowsteer is, but as I ask I look at the flowers. St. John's Wort. When I look up, the old woman isn't there. She's vanished.

"I'm about halfway up the river road when I see another old woman. She's different, but she has on a similar green suit. And this suit is like something a child might wear in the Swiss Alps. It's so foreign and *made*. She asks me the same question. *Why are you on the river road so late at night?* And again I tell her I'm on my way home. *You once took a fox in to protect it from the hunters*, she says. And I had. They'd chased it through these trees, and I opened the back door. The destruction—. The *shit* all over the walls. But the hunters couldn't enter our house—

"*I knew that fox*, the green woman tells me. *Take this posy to protect you from Crowsteer.* Again I ask who Crowsteer is, but she's vanished leaving me holding a bunch of daisies tied with a child's hair.

"By this time, the night is silver, the moon is rising. Meeting the women has scared me. The strange thing is that I can't hear the river. The path runs right alongside, but the water is silent. I can see from the current that there should be sound, and although I can hear sound from everywhere else, the black water is silent, as if the volume has been turned down on it.

"Sure enough, I meet a third old woman dressed in a much-stitched green suit. Again, she asks me the same question. *Why are you on the river road so late at night?* Again I tell her I'm on my way home. She holds out primroses. *You once rescued a fawn from a net*, she says. *That fawn was my sister.* Then she leans in. *I see you have two other posies, yet you're still on the river road. As you're clearly a fool, will you take some advice?*

"*You need to reach the Owlbridge Yew before the moon has cleared the branches. If you don't*—. This time I am looking directly at her when she vanishes. I can't explain it. She says her piece and then she is gone.

"The problem I have is that the moon is in and out of the clouds, and running would be foolhardy. So I take it steady, but it's soon obvious to me I am not going to reach the yew before the moon is above it so I start to speed up along the river road. Except I can feel the silent black water thicken beside me. I can't explain it, but hands of oil and silt are snatching out from the water. The path is holding onto my boots for a moment with every step. And then I realise I'm entering the ash trees, and every last one of them has its hand out, and because it's so dark the claws of these crow trees are black, black—

"I start to feel their touch, these shadow hands. I know that somehow what reaches for me from the water and the wood is all Crowsteer, and I panic.

"And it comes to me that I'm in a tale. Of course I'm in a tale, and it's a version of a tale I've heard all my life. So I fling the bunch of St. John's Wort over my right shoulder towards the river and shout, *Crowsteer.* I throw the daisies over my head to land on the path behind me and shout, *Crowsteer.* I throw the primroses over my left shoulder into the ash trees and shout, *Crowsteer.*

"I nearly don't make it. They have my coat. They've left scratches on my back, and my ankle is twisted. The shadows have taken hold of me, but still I reach the Owlbridge Yew before the moon clears the branches. I climb, and sit there watching the shadows scratch the air in front of the tree in fury that I slipped their grasp.

"At dawn, villagers come. One of them says, *I didn't expect to find anyone alive*, and he points to where they've brought the vicar with them. When I ask them how they knew to come out to the yew, he replies, *The river always runs silent when Crowsteer hunts.*" Peter lowered his head and repeated, "The river always runs silent when it hunts."

He'd spooked her, and he knew it. "Piss off," she said.

He laughed. "From that moment, everything was connected for me. In life. In dreams. In nature, in relationships. Whenever I walked, I felt my existence was doubled, and I was within reach of unknown things. I don't know whether escaping them earned me respect, or perhaps it was because I am a Littlegood. And it was, of course, the sixties so I was doubtless swayed by the indulgent river of *me* everyone was then swept along with.

"Elfy told you about the graves. It remains a startling experience, placing a person at the limits of the self. I remember hardly anything of the time I was away. One night I found myself a book in the grave, written on pages made of pressed leaves. In it I found spells, tales and strange diatribes against people known to the writer. *The dishonouring of a badger. A garden fork returned without one tine. An accidentally burned baby.*" He frowned. "A lot of crimes against grain and dancing. Poor dancers got the worst of the invective—

"The spells never worked and the tales were incomplete, but here and there were recipes. And one was for wild marjoram tea. And the tea takes a person right there. And so I tried it, and later shared it." He fell silent. "This is where the error lay. By whatever logic holds, my sight of the book was an invitation, but it was for myself alone. To have shared it with others was—."

He was silent for a while. When next he spoke, he whispered. "One night I was out walking when I felt the presence beside me. It was dusk. Out in the woods." He pointed. "Right there. Five minutes' walk from here. And I became lost. The path through the woods went up hills and down into valleys there are no trace of in daylight. And always a presence ahead of me, behind. As night fell, and I was getting frantic at not being able to find my way home, a woman stepped from the trees. She was dressed head to toe in black. The only colour on her was the lining of one trouser pocket, which was a deep red. Only one trouser pocket. There was no metal on her anywhere. The buttons on her suit were made of wood, and around her neck hung a bone and leather thong. I had seen it somewhere before. Somewhere both in my travels over the border, but also—. Somewhere else.

"She told me I had transgressed in sharing the secret. She said such a vision of the whole truth of nature – of the green mind – was not in my gift. I could use it myself, but I could not share it. I had to promise never to make the tea for another, and as surety for my promise, I had to offer something in return. A forfeit. A thing I must surrender if I broke my word. And I never have, from that day to this. And once I'd given that surety, I found I'd been standing in the long grass all along, and home was right there in the centre of the moonlight."

He spoke simply yet when Polly looked into his eyes, she could see how intently he was staring at her. A part of him knew, she realised, what she was there to ask. He knew this was what she wanted him to do.

"I need to understand," she told him. "To know. I need to know what happened to Tom."

"You need to feel that what happened was not your fault."

She paused. "Yes. Yes, perhaps."

"It was not your fault," he said.

Polly gave him a baleful look and ignored him. "To find out that if I'd spoken earlier the outcome might have been different. To know that another outcome was not possible."

"Another outcome was not possible."

"Peter, I need to *know* it not be told it."

He leaned forward. "I searched. Alone as I could not take another. I didn't see him."

"But Tom wouldn't have been alert for you. What connection between you would have sparked into life at your presence?"

She felt foolish saying this last, yet he didn't laugh at her. He understood what she meant; understood in his bones that such an elemental affinity as friendship and shared tribulation was exactly the kind of connection that would have an effect under the ground. This was the root of her belief that what she wanted was necessary. If Tom was there, he would make himself visible to her. And strangely, to have sight of him, to connect with him, was all she desired.

Peter knew this. He knew what she was asking. Quietly, he said, "You have no idea what I had to offer as surety."

"Your child," Polly replied.

Peter scowled. "What? No. *Jesus*, no. Of course not." His anger came out of him like a dart. "That's despicable. How the hell could you think that of me?"

In the face of his anger, Polly found no response beyond, "Robin."

"That's just a risk all families run in places where the veil is thin. That was *not* the surety I offered."

Polly tried another argument. "I've been there before. Robin made the tea. I have already been invited."

Peter shook his head. "That is not the same thing." He sounded doubtful. "The risk is too great."

"It's a reason you could offer."

"Reason?" he said. He laughed, not a kind sound. "Did you say the word *reason?*"

Polly said, "I can only ask."

The silence stretched. She let it bed in. Peter was not looking at her now. He was in the warren, his mind darting down tunnels she could not identify; whether tunnels of guilt, obligation, sorrow, pity, she did not know. In the end she realised that what she wanted him to find – what best served her interests – was none of these. She wanted his curiosity to reach him, and as she watched him think, she understood she'd known all along he would find it. She and he were linked at the *curious* level, and she knew in her bones that their curiosities resonated with each other. On another timeline, in some form they'd have been married.

When he stood, decision made, he was altered, more confident, younger somehow. He vanished into his cellar and returned with a blue glass jar. The liquid within looked oily, and its green behind blue glass looked sea-brown, poisonous. He shook the bottle and the liquid innards exploded in grit, bubbles and lengths that looked like hairs with the ability to wriggle. Here and there whole heads of flowers turned, old and gnarled, rot-bitten.

Polly was scared. She owned it. Her heartbeat was out of her grip. Her heart did not have her best interests at heart.

"What does it do?" she asked, quiet now.

Peter filled the copper-bottomed pan and put it onto the stove, clicking on a radio yet turning the music down to almost inaudible.

"I don't know," he said. "Not in a chemical sense. No doubt *psychoactive* and *psychedelic* are terms boffins would use." He busied himself with a rustic homemade teapot. Polly wondered if it was one of Elfy's creations. "At a certain point the tea's active ingredient becomes——. Well, *active*."

When hot, he poured the tea then fixed a purple cosy over the top of the pot. Cautiously, Polly began to drink.

They discussed the flavour, its sweetness and creosoty bite that was not far distant from dandelion and burdock. She remembered how it cleared her nose at the same time as settling a wheeze in her throat. The tea tasted natural and clean, which was strange considering how dirty the glass container had been.

Peter drank with his pinky out like a snail's eye. He asked about her parents, her life. Polly talked about her work, her experiences, her eye. She asked about Robin, but he had no more knowledge than Elfy. Oddly, he used the same words she'd used. *He's out there*.

She asked him about the graves, whether he was still burying people alive for an experience of death, the void. He shook his head——

"There was a Dutch film," he said. "Put paid to that. It gave people the shrieking willies."

The statement sounded like a genie had escaped his bottle and could not be put back, like the origin of childbirth, splitting the atom, the knowledge of death.

She felt close to him, more so as she felt the first lift of the wild marjoram tea. The feeling was in her feet first, then her scalp felt light. The feeling was not all pleasant: she felt slippages in her attention, and her fingers felt numb and webbed. *My fingers feel ill*, she thought and smiled.

"It doesn't taste of marjoram," she said.

He laughed, delighted. "No. You tried to make it?"

She was embarrassed. She had.

"It increases with each——. I don't know what you'd call it. Distillation? At a certain point the intoxicant effect becomes——. Animate." He looked pleased with the word. "I think of it as consciousness. The wild marjoram tea reaches consciousness. And it has agency in the world. Its consciousness can act in concert with you.

"There's more to it, of course," said Peter. "My tea goes through sixteen fortifications. A woman in Linnet has kept a marjoram still steeping forty years. In its natural state—. Its *sorry* state—." He opened his mouth to signify but not sound laughter. He poured her more tea. "In its natural state it's good for digestion, mental clarity. I add orbody, common burdock, or clot-burr, hurr-burr. An anti-scorbutic *Iberis* known as bitter candy-tuft or clown's mustard. God, it makes me so happy to say the words!

"The tea opens up the interior. Like all humans, you're filled with closed rooms. Did you know the first time a child sees a buttercup, she only senses it bottom-up? Colour, scent, shape. Ever after, the brain meets this sensing halfway. Top-down processing fills in the name, facts, folklore, *science*." He pulled a face. "In truth, we only ever *see* a buttercup once, and then that door closes. Until now—."

He closed her ill fingers around the mug. "I'm scared," she said.

"Why wouldn't you be?" said Peter. "The green mind is not your friend. I thought you understood that, Polly—

"Have you ever wondered why children are so rapt by folk tales? Why they insist on their being repeated accurately? It's because they recognise their truth, and not just their truth but their reality. A folk tale has consciousness. It glows with pleasure when you hear it. Everything does. *Things* glow with pleasure when you notice them."

Peter was right. Everything she looked at glowed with pleasure now, brighter or dimmer depending on its form. A pot of basil on the sill was ridiculous. The green was so vivid it looked false. The words, however, seemed to blink off in her head as if a switch had been flipped on nouns as they came into her mind, clunked with a cudgel as each name popped out of its brain hole. The *green* glowed and the *longer* glowed and the *grainy* glowed and the *clear* glowed, but the *whistled shape* did not glow very brightly, and neither did the *handled green-bottom* on the stove. Music dribbled from a *buttony-black* that didn't glow at all.

"Things that are made by people glow," she concluded aloud, "and things made by machines don't glow. Things that just *are* glow brightest of all."

Peter threw his head back and howled with laughter. The ribbed noise made her more anxious.

They went outside. In the shadows under the sill an enormous creature stood and shivered upright.

"Burgess," whispered Peter. "You remember Polly."

She'd forgotten the dog was black to the eyes, then she opened her mouth to lick her hand and she saw the deep red pocket of her mouth.

How old is this dog? thought Polly, then the switch on the word *dog* clicked off and she'd no idea what the shadow that walked with them into the woods was called.

Soon there were trees, hamlets seen on far hillsides, candles carried deep in the woods as if orange light were thread stitching into black cloth. Music oozed from the wood. They walked through a singing horse fair, stalls filled with games and food around the main place of the auction. A choir of Exmoor ponies were making a handsome fist of *Billy Budd*. She went to pull Peter's arm to get him to look, but Polly was alone and had no recollection of who she'd been reaching for.

A man off to the side was walking with a woman dressed all in velvet black with one deep red trouser pocket. He was the man from that house. The glow house in the grass wood circle. The man who made her the tea. Soon another man was there, a gentleman she recognised who pulled a paper bag from a trouser pocket that opened wide and red, and which he flicked open with a thumbnail like a silver butterknife.

"Bee?" he asked.

An unknown length of time later, the gentleman handed her onto a boat with the taste of honey in her mouth. Polly recognised that she was underground, in one of the rooms that grew laterally from the main trunk, a water room. As the gentleman stepped back through the wood that led to the trunk, she saw a coffin pulled up towards the ground. The window over the face plate in the coffin was turned away, hidden from her as the coffin twisted upwards.

Her pilot was a woman with luminous eyes who gave her name as Chittermink. Her skin smelled of oranges and cloves. "Sit on the bread oven," she whispered to Polly.

Polly pushed her bottom onto the warm oven, heat feeding up through her, arse to crown, and when she next looked behind her there was no sign of land. They were on the open night sea, and as the boat sailed on, Polly slowly relaxed. Chittermink did not speak. She lay on her back staring at the stars above, smoking a curved hand-rolled cigar. The smoke she exhaled shot past Polly's head in an instant. Polly recognised this meant they were travelling at an incredible rate of knots, yet Chittermink smoked idly, her bare foot resting on the handle of the tiller, which curiously was at the front of the boat, her loose slit skirt fallen open to show the length of her thigh.

Now and then the bread oven Polly was sat on gave a hiccup and a loaf slid out the back where sharp-toothed fishes ate their way to the insides causing the crust to wriggle wildly as it sped out of sight.

Once she'd noticed this, she began to see all manner of creatures beneath the surface of the water. Extraordinary, half human, bright-eyed. At regular intervals, a creature slid huge beneath her, featureless and grey but for the eyes and a tail like a pick axe. This was visible because in the depths was light, and at the bottom of the sea was an underwater country, villages surrounded by fields, high hedges, rivers running out towards mills and farms. It was too distant to see figures. Polly felt as though she were high in a balloon at cloud level, the scene far beneath her busy, full of rustic industry and mischief. She was still rapt with the vision below when she realised the boat was slowly coming to a halt.

Chittermink was standing now. As the boat rocked to a full stop, Polly joined her at the prow. Polly was small but the woman was tiny, and now they were close she saw Chittermink was completely *other*. It was like a trick of film, as if they might be similar sizes but the difference between them had been altered to put them side by side. The great woman, Mossycoat, came to mind then. Her height and bulk pressing Polly down had felt to be a similar assemblage of realities of different size. This phrase stuck with Polly. *Our realities are of different sizes.*

There was a quality to Chittermink that was sharp, and it wasn't her teeth or ears or knifey feet but a skeletal quality, as if her bones were lengths of broken glass. Polly recalled the last words of Tom's mother, Emese. *There were riders. Sharp riders.*

The boat circled idly. "Where are we?"

"The boat of a king comes," replied Chittermink. She pointed at the moon. "A dance is on the cards. Might you kick the oven?"

After a pause, Polly did so. With a choke, a loaf slid into the water and floated alongside. The sharp-fish, heads so swollen with teeth they looked like malignant tadpoles, bit their way in and hollowed the loaf out in seconds.

The tiny woman got a gaff pole through one of the holes and lifted it high, the fish abandoning the rising loaf, which now looked like a bread dolls' house. Angling the pole, this house slid down to Chittermink who forced a fish hook through the loaf roof before giving it to Polly to hold. The hollow loaf stank. Where the fish had wriggled inside, the bread had been saturated with oil, which Chittermink now lit and the loaf glowed with blue fire.

As the flames crept into a glowing ball, Polly saw more of the sea. Approaching was a boat in the shape of a crescent, the distance between the two horns about that of a football field, curving toward them to gather Chittermink's boat within the great turning arc. It was hard to believe this floating raft was possible, but as they were caught in the calm pool between the crescent horns, Polly saw how the centre of the arc was filled with houses built up one atop the other, not one of them the same shape or size. Between the houses ran steep wooden steps that scampered over roofs and through dwellings. Those streets reminded her of Annesdock on the coast, a thrown-together place. Even from a distance she saw the dwellings all touched, and where they touched was a door so the inhabitants could wind through from house to house. Polly watched as Chittermink steered them close to a jetty sticking out from the centre of the boat of the king. The jetty was lined with tubs of daffodils, and a curious insistent music rumbled the timbers of the enormous wooden crescent.

"They're dancing," Polly said.

"Naturally," replied Chittermink.

She gestured to the jetty with an open palm, and as Polly walked towards the dance, crowds of little folk pushed past her, hungry for the pilot's bread.

At the end of the jetty, the light was bright so she blew out her loaf lantern and set it on the planks. Rodents darted in. The crisp sounds of mice feet on the fishy toast inside made her smile.

The structures at sea level were filled with light and music. Bodies were everywhere, dancing but most houses looked like mosh pits. Picking the least fighty, Polly stepped in and joined the dance. The room was rough, boyish. To enter took courage, but only the kind of courage that trusted that, despite a knock or two, she'd come out cared for and only minimally scathed.

Immediately, she was fed. A woman standing on the shoulders of an upright pig pushed something potatoey and good into her mouth. Beer was taken, but by then she'd been danced up to the first floor into a house at the rear of the crescent that stared out at the featureless sea and the moon hanging low in the centre of the huge open window. The dance never stopped so even though she wanted to stay and look out at that exquisite vision of the sea at night, the bodies of the folk carried her on, on—

The music was music she knew and did not know. It was folk music, melancholic, plaintive, yet with a driving force that felt like the blood beat of embarrassment in her face. Now and then she seemed to catch a line of something she knew – *Monks Gate, On Yonders Hill, The Boys of Annesdock* – but the tune was not quite right, as if only a kissing cousin to a folk song from the lands she knew.

The dance lived in her feet, partly because the dancers were so thick their movement was in a sense the same. They flowed in a liquid, most reaching only to Polly's breasts with here and there giants both fat and thin who formed pillars around which the dance flowed. The dance was an oil that flowed upwards. They danced over roofs and through windows, even up ladders and down the sides of buildings. Her body surrendered completely to the flow, yet occasionally, like a log in a river, she stuck for a moment and her mind gathered, suddenly in solitude and aware of her surroundings before she was hooked back in.

There were dark rooms lit with one candle where Polly stared in at the jamb to see a grey baby being born, feet first and arse up, a perfect fern growing out of its anus. The candle-lit birth was shepherded by three sharp women, each bald with a wig made of straw tied in a top knot jammed on their heads. She was caught again and flowed upward and upward—

—a bar where the customers paid by standing on a chair and allowing the giant barmaid to finger out their bellybutton felt, which she weighed on a set of scales where the weights were feathers of different birds. "Shy of three duck feathers," she muttered, serving the man his ale and giving him change in gold. A hand took Polly's and dealt her back into the dance—

—a tailor at a high house was working at a collar the size of a whale's flipper, the button a slice through the bole of a tree. The floor dropped away beneath him to show a shaft clear to the boat bowels. A suit forty foot long was hanging on an anchor sunk into the ceiling. At each level below, tailors reached into the shaft to work on their portion of the suit: lapels below, then sleeves and pockets, cuffs, down, down into the hull far below.

"Who's the suit for?" asked Polly.

The tailor peered up at her. Pointing to the floor, which Polly read as being underwater, he whispered, "The horseman."

A giant picked her up and screwed her bodily back into the centre of the dance.

At the top of the boat was a bridge between two high houses. The far house was larger than the others, a balloon swaying above its roof. The dancers went over the bridge then vanished to the lower levels, a river of folk flowing downward now they'd reached the apex. Polly clung to the side of the bridge until the last of the dancers had descended and she was alone at last.

The scene was a wonder. Far below on the softly swelling sea, no land in sight, boats and rafts were gathered within the wooden bay. The night all around was blue-black, the moon behind her illuminating the scene. She watched for what felt like hours.

The boats were trading, a barter market where each boat and raft shared its wares. They pulled alongside each other as they traded. Polly could tell Chittermink's boat by the tiny spud of her bread oven. At this high point, the whole of the crescent village was visible, alive with music, dance, candlelight, yet the flotilla was slow and silent, protected by the greater calm in the bay formed between the horns of the crescent craft. Behind them lay the horizon and stars. Polly felt extraordinary, perfectly at peace, wellness giddy in her limbs as if she'd eaten nothing but vegetables for days.

From the big dwelling, a man descended the wooden staircase and stepped onto the bridge.

"You're Polly," he said. "It's wonderful you could come."

His voice was low, seductive. The other folk had spoken less well, some only able to manage a beetly tumble of consonants, or a language that sounded full of feathers. As he came closer, she could see why. It was a younger Peter, his hair full and his body strong. She'd never seen a more beautiful man, and the core of his beauty was the daft fact of his ears, which stuck out from his head at right angles, lobeless, egg shaped. Elfy's ears. This was their son, and though he was dressed no more lavishly than the others – a rustic suit with wooden buttons, no metal – she knew this was who Chittermink had meant when she had said it was the boat of the king. She'd no idea what his given name might be. Almost certainly he'd never had one, not in truth. It would have been Robin, but he was not Robin.

"I'm looking for Tom."

"I know you are," he said. "There's not another reason for you to be here."

He smiled. His beauty reached right into her and took a seat quietly in her lower belly. She wanted to kiss him.

"Would you tell me where he is?"

"I've already told Chittermink where to find him. He's on his island with his queen. Come to my home," he said. "You won't be able to leave 'til dawn anyway."

In that instant, Polly was sticky with terror. "That woman—."

The king shook his head. "Mossycoat has business elsewhere," he told her. "She won't be back until tomorrow." He smiled again, a grin that got into her head in a way that was both enchanting and infuriating; a grin with fingers. "Come," he whispered.

Although it was the largest dwelling on the boat, his house was still small. Boys took off her shoes and cleaned her toes with chamois leather cloths. One boy was enchanting, about six years old and adorable: pouty of belly, his lower lip stuck out with importance as he handed over soap and cloths and squares of soft, pressed petals for her hands and face. They led her to a room with a toilet and a four-footed bath already full and steaming. The look of it was enticing.

When she turned, the boys were standing there armed with brushes, flannels, the oldest wearing two hessian mittens ready for scrubbing her skin.

She laughed. "Nope," she said, and pushed them out of the door.

After the bath, she found her clothes had been taken. No one was there. Curiously, she felt no shame and, naked, she walked towards the elevated level of the wooden house. She recalled her grandmother's phrase for being clean. *I feel like a new pin.*

The king of the boat was up the stairs lying on the bed. The room was open on all sides to the night air. It was a four-poster room. At the edges of each sill burned fire for heat.

There was no hesitancy in her. She'd desired the king since she'd seen him. She shuffled her bottom onto the bed so her head fell next to his, their feet facing away from each other.

"Where are the boys?" she asked.

"I have sent them away."

She turned to face him. "Will they return?"

His lips were so full, parted only a little. His eyes were green. He gave a little chirrup, and there was movement above. Through a skylight she'd not known was there, a huge mass of black feathers moved, and a black claw gripped and tugged a wooden lever, the strain of this action opening the great black bird's cloaca, which flashed deep red. Slowly the room ascended, lifted by the balloon for a hundred feet before the chain connecting it to the house caught, and the room swayed on this tether under the moonlight.

"How long have you lived here?" she asked.

The king frowned. "I was born here."

"You look like someone I know."

"Everybody does," he whispered.

Polly could feel the blood thud in her groin.

"How are you the king?"

"Through the worship of another."

"The woman who chased me all that time ago? Mossycoat."

"Yes, but it wasn't so long ago."

"And she cannot find us here?"

"Oh, she could climb that rope so fast your boiled egg wouldn't be cooked," he said. "And she is understanding of the need for the occasional wedding. Between the fields you know and the fields we know." Without moving, he pushed his lips out, stretching until they were hilariously, hesitantly able to kiss her nose. "Most likely she'd only blind you. But she's far away tonight."

Polly kissed him back. "Who's your mother?" she whispered.

"A scullery maid from Churchtown."

"Who's your father?"

"The north wind."

She reached over her hand and gently ran her fingers over the arch of his ear. "I know your father," she whispered.

"Everyone knows my father. He reminds them to wear a coat. He can be quite boring about it."

"Have you ever been to my world?"

"No. Mossycoat tells me all about it. She goes there often. She says the light is bad and the water hard and none of the creatures can speak. Even the trees talk above your head."

"This is true," she said. "Everything you say is true."

The blood in her veins was like a mob rioting in the streets. She rolled herself up and stared down at him, his upside down face so sweet and calm and patient—

In sex, she had never been particularly active. Here, it was both within reach and needful for the king was hesitant. Polly marvelled at his skin, which was soft and scented and *different*, he seemed similarly surprised by her. It was an hour before urgency came, yet even then she had the sense they were both happy with tumbling over each other like puppies, love making that was clumsy and lovely, playful. It reminded her of being young. She felt young.

After the king had burned the silk cloth they'd used to clean themselves, he stood at the corner post, his bottom a temptation for her teeth in the moonlight. Beyond him, the night sea stretched to the horizon. The cool air on her skin was delight incarnate.

Polly slept.

Hours later, she heard scratching and felt movement, and the black bird climbed down past the open window where the sun was rising. The bird was the size of a bear, covered in black feathers apart from the head, which was encased in reptilian leather. All was black, even to the eyes, and then it was gone, and moments later she felt the floating room descend, presumably as the bird clawed them down to their anchorage.

The boys were furious when they clambered in. The look of affront on the six-year-old's face made her laugh. She wondered if he'd been holding her clean clothes in such a sulky way all night. As the other boys busied themselves running her bath and arranging her breakfast, she looked out at the sunrise wondering where the king was, for she had woken alone. It was entirely possible that he had fallen from the room to his death, or flown away into the night. Somehow it didn't matter.

Chittermink was waiting for her on the jetty. The residents of the great boat were all asleep, drunk still. The only morning people around were gangs of boys and girls mopping up spilled beer.

Chittermink said nothing. She resumed her loose drape at the prow once the boat was under way, smoking her cigar and gazing over the water.

In no time, they came to an island covered in trees. The island was remarkable to see for there was not even a beach. The trees hung over the water, every last inch of coast used to anchor their last root.

Chittermink could not land – there was no jetty – so she sailed to a large limb and held them steady.

"The one you seek serves his queen at the centre. You'll find the trees have grown into a path that will take you there." Chittermink took the cigar from her mouth and blew the smoke into the leaves above her. "Do not touch the ground on this island."

"If I fall?"

"Do not fall."

"Do they know I'm coming?"

"The Bird will have told him."

Polly knew from how she said it that the word *bird* was capitalised. She paused. "It was lovely to meet you," she said. "Will I see you again?"

"No. You've been here too long already. You'll thread back into your own world soon." She hesitated. "It was lovely to meet you too."

Polly clambered onto the limb. By the time she was awkwardly standing, Chittermink was in the distance, her boat centred on the rising sun.

The woman was right, however. Although the way was precarious, a path was navigable over the trees' larger limbs. The canopy was thick, and thick with seabirds. The way was beautiful, with here and there hollows piled with dried food and clay flagons for travellers, seats grown into the wood.

None of the animals that lived in the trees were truly wild. Squirrels did not run from her, and she had a sense larger creatures were moving deep in the branches where the path did not go and the light did not reach: moving strengths both deliberate and watchful. The path rose gradually until there were moments when on tiptoe she could see through the canopy to the expanse of the island lonely on a featureless sea. She pushed on, footsteps increasingly confident on the smooth wooden path that wound up and down and from side to side.

Soon, where the wood was thickest, the wide limb ended in a small wooden door. She knocked gently, and the door opened onto a dark, dark room. "Come in, Polly," said Tom.

There were no lights in the tree house. All was sunk in gloom. What little she could see of Tom showed a man much like the king had been, tall and strong, perhaps with harder skin. His movement was slower, however, more like that of a soldier. She wanted to cry.

She followed him into a large dark room. He was still in shadow. To Polly, it seemed the room was filled with smoke.

Tom's room reminded her of Mrs Tarr's house. The inside was gloomy and filled with deep brown furniture, no ornaments. The darkness was near complete so the chests and chairs and tables were mostly shadow, like a Victorian drawing room viewed through blue glass. On a wall she could see a board full of bells. It resembled a flat carillon. There were dozens of them all different sizes and presumably ringing with a different tone, and she guessed they were there for summoning Tom.

Straight ahead she saw a thick tapestry across a wooden frame, few details visible. The cloth allowed no light through so she could not tell if it covered a window or a wall. In front of the tapestry were two chairs.

"Is there a light?" she asked.

"The only light here is daylight," he replied. "I'll make us some tea."

While Tom was elsewhere, she tried to make out what was on the tapestry. It was huge, about twenty foot wide by eight foot tall, and a wave throbbed through it as though a breeze were blowing on the other side, yet it was too heavy for her to lift a corner to see what might be beyond.

Instead she looked to see what details she could make out on the surface, but it was bewildering. There was a tree not unlike the one she'd just climbed through with figures embedded within dressed in rustic clothes and covered with flowers. She walked along the length of the tapestry slowly, careful not to trip over anything in the darkness. She made out a fox on her back in a bower, waited on by boys and girls half her size, a woman flossing the vixen's teeth with sprigs of mint. A ring of dancers wound around an ancient standing stone, the path of the dancers running through an upright stone ring they had to duck to step through. She saw sleeping figures – human-sized – on hay bales with gold falling from their pockets, little folk on spinning wheels and millstones.

The work was fine, and at times she felt she knew the faces. They were faces she'd seen growing up on the farms that were passed down from generation to generation, yet even the strange little folk in their suits of blue looked like people she knew. With a start, she saw a detail at the far end of the tapestry that showed boys clinging to the backs of cows, almost racing them, each figure woven so finely she could see where the barbs halfway down their thumbs were dug like spurs into the cows' flanks while the riders had sunk their triangular teeth into the bovine necks to feed.

"Sit."

Polly sat. Not to see Tom was frustrating. His voice was the same, but the body she could dimly make out in the dark was not. He had a man's body as she had a woman's. She took the tea he offered, wondering how to begin to speak, wondering what in fact it was she wanted to say when Tom said—

"I always thought I would see you again. Not to have had that as our ending. I wanted to thank you. That time after mum—. I was so lonely."

"You visited me. In the dark room when I was bandaged. I wanted to say sorry. That last time we spoke. I shouted at you. I really shouted."

"Did you?" he said. "I don't remember that."

"How is it you stayed here?" she asked.

"I was brought here. A girl had seen me and asked for me to be brought. She asked for me and I was given to her. I think I told you that."

"I don't know what to say."

"Nothing to say. We wed, and I learned how life is here. There were—. Adjustments. Yet there is never a moment here when I'm not sunk in wonder."

"You don't miss the other world?"

He shook his head. "I was sixteen. I'm not sure how much I really knew of it to miss it."

He took a sip of tea. Polly did the same, wary that it might be unwise, but it tasted like sweet chamomile.

"I was lonely then," he said. "Until you came along, I was lonely. Here I'm never lonely. I have my queen. And every day there's dancing—

"I have a use here. And I've come to an understanding that not to be of use is one of the worst fates that can befall a human being."

"What is your use?"

"I serve."

Polly paused. "You serve your queen?"

Tom pushed himself into the shadows. He pulled a lever, and a mechanism that sounded full of cogs, clockwork, ropes and weights was set in motion. A shudder ran through the tapestry, and as a mammoth weight sank into the trees beneath them, the tapestry began to rise.

Outside was a village of houses built high in the canopy of trees, circular, leading down to a central wooden structure. Thick limbs formed paths to this structure like spokes in a bicycle wheel. Polly stood to look, and found there was no glass, just the edge of the frame and the trunks Tom's house stood on. The forest floor was lost in the darkness below.

"What's down there?"

"The ground belongs to the horseman. Keep away from the edge."

"Who is the horseman?"

Tom did not reply. When it was clear that he was not going to answer, Polly pointed to the low tree houses that formed a huge ring around the central wooden palace. Tom's house was in this ring.

"Who lives in these houses?"

"The queen has many husbands and wives."

"And they all have tapestries." Many of the great windows were open as she could see figures moving about inside. "What would happen to me if they knew I was here? That I could see them?"

"I think you know that, Polly."

There were small dwellings dotted along the limbs, smoke tumbling upward from bakers and blacksmiths and cheesemongers. A glass bulb filled with liquid fizzed on a thatched roof, the bulb easily ten foot in diameter. There were houses hung *underneath* the limbs, rocking on ropes as thick as a man's leg. In the windows she saw little folk asleep, working, children playing and everywhere foxes and birds. Yet all roads led to the centre and all dwellings faced the wooden palace, a panopticon.

She watched a child pull a wheel of cheese along a branch, the wheel twice the size of his own head, and a girl walking low under the weight of an armful of logs.

"Everything goes to the centre," she muttered.

The wooden palace was lower than the wall of houses that ringed it. Polly could look down on the games courts, palace buildings, bowers, and a patch of lawn that seemed grown on a net.

In the middle of this bouncing lawn was a four poster bed in the sunlight, twenty foot on a side, on which lay a woman. She wasn't that far away and Polly could see how completely beautiful she was, fat and naked on her bed filled with fruit, which rolled to touch her body, and when she shifted the fruit rolled off into the trees far below. Wandering over the sheets were barefoot children, their shoes placed in a line at the foot, serving the queen.

"Why did you come here?" asked Tom.

"I don't know."

Her voice sounded desolate. There were too many reasons that were footling and none weighty enough that she could use, and the trivial reasons could not be gathered to make a respectable mass.

"I don't know," she repeated.

Tom came from the shadows to stand next to her. She dared not look at him. "So, another question, why now?"

In the distance the queen rolled on her back. A girl filled the queen's bellybutton with the smallest mound of soil then pressed in a pea shoot. At her other end, a boy poured a line of cream directly into her throat from a porcelain jug. Polly felt a pulse of anger near her temple.

Why now?

"I have this recurring dream," she told him. "I'm in a theatre doing a reading or something. The audience is in darkness. And you stand up and interrupt me, correct something I've said. *That's not right,* you say. *You said that wrong.* And I'm so delighted to see you, I just smile at you, but that makes you furious. Spitting with fury. And the more you shout and scream, the happier I am because I've seen you again. You're right there in front of me—

"I want something new in my life, Tom. Something different. And this needs to be finished. I'm happy carrying any guilt. Any sorrow. I don't know. Whatever weight I need to carry forward, I'm happy to carry it. But——. I need to know the nature of the weight." She paused. "I don't know if that makes any sense."

"I understand. But I wonder if there is another reason. To come here at all is to be wedded here. We were wed here when first we came. You might move forward all you like, but you need to accept this place is inside you. It's in your blood. If they count your bones when you're dead, you'll be one short."

"I couldn't stay here," Polly said.

"I would not allow it."

"Are you happy?"

Tom replied, "I am happy."

She looked up at him, and with a shock that turned her skin stiff she saw his eyes were made of wood, polished and beautifully fitted to his empty sockets. There was a soft *shh* sound when he blinked. She couldn't stop herself saying, "Oh, your eyes!"

Tom put his hand on her arm. "It's not as bad as it must seem," he said. "I can see everything the trees see." He tapped his head. "In here. But I can't see anything I see, and the trees cannot see me because I am a stranger here and will always be so." He pointed to a distant tree. "I can see this room from that tree there, but the room is empty. No one is standing here."

"I hate that woman," she hissed.

Tom smiled wide. "The queen can be cruel. She can be kind. She can be a dick, if I'm honest."

Polly was laughing when a movement caught her eye. If she was standing at six on the wooden dial, at two o'clock a tiny baby connected with the lip of the great viewing frame in the house where it lived. He teetered for a moment – *No!* – before falling forward, down into the lightless depths.

Screaming came, slitherings from below, and a sound like a man biting into a toothsome apple echoed off the trees. The child's wails were cut off instantly.

"One has fallen," said Tom.

"Is there no hope?" asked Polly, appalled.

"No," replied Tom.

The sounds of feeding grew louder, and along the boughs of the queen's fief the folk came out to witness in horrified quiet the lost child's dismemberment.

Improbably, given how much blood was likely in a toddler, a line of blood shot into the air and lashed onto the queen's bed linen. Her *tut* was louder than the great bite that had ended the child's life.

"I am needed," Tom said. "The queen will be upset."

Already there were children darting along the boughs weighed down with clean linen.

"What happens? What happens now?"

"A wake," said Tom, moving towards the door. "The queen must be consoled for her loss. The candles are already going out into the trees."

Tom was right. Boys were carrying unwieldy candles, arms scarcely able to go round their girth. When they reached the trunks, giants took and sat the candles on smooth ledges on the outer trees.

"But the child——."

"Polly, we have no time. You are already on your way home. The tea started your journey."

Just then a tone sounded on the wall of bells. "I am of use," said Tom. "Never forget, Polly, we were given a vision of a new world. We never returned completely but that's because we could not. You always leave something of yourself behind."

"That's true of any place."

"Of course." He smiled. "And you always take something away with you. You got what you came for."

Tom walked through the door and closed it behind him. By the time she reached the door and opened it again to step through, it was evening and she was in the long grass by the false graves at the Littlegood house. In front of her was the grave called *A Hare*.

It was night. All around she sensed figures were in the trees and standing in the long grass, hidden but present.

She headed towards the house, but a figure was there before her, a barrel of a man about her height, full of hair and grey malice, his eyes with almost no white. It was only when he smiled, showing triangular teeth, that she realised it was Robin.

Terror flooded her, but she dared not reject his beckoning finger and followed him out towards the walled garden behind the studio where he and Tom had played French cricket. He held the gate open for her, but stayed outside, rubbing himself against the post.

The hedges were high, but she could see a shape there in the gloom, seven foot tall and engaged in cleaning a silver length of light. The figure was Mossycoat, and the passing of a cloud let moonlight in to illuminate the woman in full.

At her feet lay a red shape in front of the stone table. Polly wanted to run but could not. To do so might signal to Mossycoat that Polly could see her, and she knew what that meant. Slowly Polly forced herself closer, pretending she couldn't see anything in the darkness.

The red shape was a body, covered in blood and curled in on itself. It looked like pain had taken all awareness from the figure at her feet apart from the green eyes which stared unseeing at Mossycoat's ankles.

"What's happened?" Polly said, talking to the figure.

Mossycoat heard her. Polly held still. To ignore the enormous figure in front of her took all her strength and will, but she knew she could not let on that she could see the giant. Mossycoat bent down, bloody to the elbows, and sniffed at Polly's face, staring her in the eyes. Filled with terror, Polly let her eyes wander over Mossycoat's face, careful not to allow her gaze to snag on the woman's scrutiny.

"Peter," said Polly, "why are you out here alone?"

Mossycoat sniffed her. Polly held her ground.

Robin at the gate broke the spell. He loosed a beetly clatter of consonants. Mossycoat glared at him.

Polly watched her pick up a mound of matter from the stone table. It looked like a wet sheet – one side red, the other side white – but it wasn't until Mossycoat held it aloft and shook it loose that Polly realised it was Peter Littlegood's skin, sliced off with the silver flensing knife.

"It's true, Robin. I *do* have my forfeit," muttered Mossycoat sadly. She pushed her thumb through the skin's anus, wiggling her thumb so hard the skin wriggled. "But look at the state of it," she said. "It's full of holes."

Polly dared not move until they were gone. Now that she understood what Peter had given as surety, she was beyond horror. She knew she had to comfort him in some way, so she leaned over to where he was bent into a foetal position and placed her hand on his shoulder to roll him onto his back. Her salt touch fell on raw meat, and he screamed, not seeing her, locked in the coffin of his pain until his blood had run into the grass and soil and he was dead.

From the shadows, Burgess gently took the man's neck in her jaws and pulled him into the darkness of the long grass. The dead man's heels being dragged on the ground sounded like sands in an hourglass. When the red, red feet had vanished into the long grass, Polly fled to her car.

The days afterwards were sunk in a shock Polly could not process, and there was a return of the blindness in her eye that her drops could not fix, or fixed only for a few minutes until the vision in that eye dimmed again until she saw only flickering points of light in what might have been a forest.

Although she wanted to, she couldn't leave the peninsula at once. There was still some business she needed to close with her parents' house, but also she needed to visit Elfy, and there was an evening where she told the woman of the boat of the king, and Peter—

"It would always have ended like that," Elfy said. "You shouldn't have told me of the king though."

"I thought—. To know for certain."

"No," replied Elfy. "No, it gives me nothing but pain." She paused. "That was always part of my pain. I could never travel there. For some reason, I wasn't recognised. My passage was not approved. My presence was not wanted. *I* was not wanted."

Polly left the next morning. It seemed clear she would never see this woman again.

In this she was wrong, however. As time went on, the terror bedded in until she feared for her sanity. All was horror, and the horror built day on day until her mind sheared like slate—

Fleeing home brought no relief, so after the wholesale abandonment of her life – her job, her friends, her house – she ended up getting on a plane to the furthest destination she could enter without waiting for a visa. She entered Thailand with nothing but money, far distant from the world she knew, and even though she was still waking in fright from the vision of Mossycoat dangling a man's skin by the heels, she found herself gradually calming day by day until one afternoon, as a kindly man in Mahasarakham showed her dinosaur bones, she realised she'd not come on in months. Whatever else, Tom had been right. She'd taken the great night with her, and some golden, long-boned, jug-eared sperm had connected with her dud-eyed, short-legged, bookish egg to make a child.

As she sat on the bus through the dusty countryside, longing for sundown and the thundersome crickets of evening, she knew she would have to see Elfy again, months if not years hence, to introduce her to her grandchild, her blood.

When the child was born, Polly called her Sylvia, which is of course where I come in—

Notes and Acknowledgements

Wild Marjoram Tea contains language and attitudes accurate for the time, but which are no longer in use. No offence is intended.

The book draws on a wide range of British folklore. Katharine Briggs's work is a major influence, as is the myriad wealth of English and Scottish song, and some of the inspirations for this book, notably *Young Tambling* and *Crooker*, will be recognised from those sources. Sylvia Townsend Warner is rootstock—

Towards the end, Tom speaks an idea first heard in Kurt Vonnegut's *The Sirens of Titan* and, later, Smog's *To Be of Use*.

Firefay's *Tales of Monsters and Fairies* and Belbury Poly's *The Gone Away* were musical staples through the later parts of the writing.

Thanks to John Logan, Lindy Webster, Victoria Wainwright, Alison Brown, Robert Walsh and Miranda Waugh, owl-pedant.